Money
Land

R.S. Guthrie

To my mother,
who wanted to
"be a writer."
You were, Mom.
A damn fine one.

ACKNOWLEDGEMENTS

First, you don't write a novel about Wyoming and not acknowledge the genuine, unique, hard-working, tough-loving people of the land itself. I have many friends there still, both American and Native American. The latter know how I feel about history, but every one of you has a pride that no one will ever be able to take away. I say with the deepest respect: I admire you more than any group of people I've known. You are the toughest, hardest-working men and women and your love for Wyoming and the land I will never tire of witnessing.

To my editor, Russell Rowland, an acclaimed, published writer in his own right: I've yet to find such a fine editor, nor one who is so adept at making my writing better with even the tiniest of suggested changes. You, sir, are brilliant and I owe a debt of gratitude to you because you understand the place from whence these Pruett books come.

To my proofreader, beta reader, friend, confidant, and most importantly to the book, an honest reader and commenter, Gail Gentry. Like Russell, you always have the perfect suggestions and your proofing is eagle-eyed. Your forthcoming novel will show the world how much talent you've been gifted.

To my wife, Amy, who has read every novel I write more times in full and in part than any other living human being, thank you for believing in me but most for being by my side. The further we get in this journey to that porch swing the more I depend on you and you have supported my dream from the beginning. I love you.

To bestselling author and friend, Russell Blake. You keep me on the correct road. Your advice is like gold bullion, your mind as sharp as any I know, and your work ethic and talent undeniable and amazing. Thank you for everything.

And to the readers. I've said it before but will continue to reaffirm it: you are the lifeblood to the writer. And for me, every letter, each word, all the pages—they are ultimately for you. When you humble authors by reading their work and further by telling others, you literally help the writer survive to write another day. You are so very much appreciated.

Preface

I don't normally write a preface to my books, but I recently had a reader pick up the second book in a series and read it first. She loved the story but felt she would have enjoyed it more had she known the history of the returning characters better. I thought that was fair—once a writer has eight or nine books in a series, perhaps the need to inform the reader they are picking up book number four or five becomes less important, but when there are only two or three in the series, I decided it would be the proper thing to do to let you, the reader (or potential reader) know that this is the second in the **James Pruett Mystery/Suspense** series, so if you haven't read the first one (*Blood Land*), you might consider it.

I do my best to give enough background story in any "series" book that a reader should be okay if they haven't read the prior book(s), but I wanted to respect the woman who took the time to comment enough to put this preface in book number two of this series.

In fact, my editor, Russell Rowland, told me that Alfred Hitchcock distinguished Mysteries by two different styles. The first was the traditional "whodunnit". From page one the reader had no idea who the bad guy or gal was. I likened that to a boardgame of Clue. The second style he deemed "Suspense". That would be where you pretty much knew (or thought you knew) who did what, but it was the *getting there* and the twists along the way that made the read a good one.

I tend to write the latter. I love twists. I also love putting something right in the reader's face and daring them to believe otherwise. Because of this, however, I do work hard to make each book in a series capable (hopefully) of standing on its own as best it can.

For me, as a reader—and being a character-driven author—it is the relationships I develop with returning protagonists, ancillary characters, villains, etc. that make me want to read the books in order.

Whatever your preference, I certainly hope you enjoy *Money Land* as much as I enjoyed writing it. Cheers.

Rob (R.S.) Guthrie, 2012

"Well, I am no thief,
but a man can go wrong
when he's busted
The food that we canned last summer
is gone and I'm busted
The fields are all bare
and the cotton won't grow,
Me and my family
got to pack up and go,"
Ray Charles, *Busted*

R.S. GUTHRIE

Chapter 1

MARK COULEE sat in the cramped, sweltering office in the near-deserted airport outside Tempe, Arizona, lines of sweat mixing with fear mixing with a sad feeling of complete bewilderment. A scorpion scuttled across the open, filthy floor, making a break for some kind of freedom until Mark stomped on it with his boot. The pattern of insides and scorpion blood formed a design that looked like the Star of David and Mark thought for a moment about his father.

His dad had been a sometimes-practicing Jew who was what most people call a *hardworking man*, which meant he spent the bulk of his life working for a company that could not have cared less about who he was, what his dreams might be, how beautiful and loving his wife was, or what was really going on inside his head. He lined the pockets of the corporate executive pigs and all the stockholders and then was laid off unceremoniously without pension, severance, or self-respect.

Mark's dad committed suicide. He shot himself through the temple with a .22 pistol he'd never fired before the day he left the world and he did it in a place and time when Mark, then seventeen, would find him lying in a surprisingly trifling pool of blood, the lesser caliber slug having caromed around inside his head like a tiny pinball.

He'd never been particularly proud of Mark even though Mark had managed to pull good enough grades to get into any college he wanted and had won several full academic scholarships.

Mark wondered how it was a man woke up one day and found his life resembling that of someone completely different than he set out to be. Perhaps that was the day a man considered turning a gun he'd never fired once in his entire life on *himself*.

No, that was NOT the day. Mark had already faced *that* day—the day *his* company laid him off—and he'd not considered committing suicide (later when he pondered the "why?" he just figured he got his will to live from his mother).

But he'd considered since then that he *ought* to have killed himself that day; instead Mark was now a man who he'd never dreamed he could become; a man he no longer recognized when he walked past a mirror; and a man who harbored thoughts of things he'd never imagined before all this. It wasn't a physical or psychological condition by any stretch. It wasn't depression, or low self-esteem, or unfulfilled expectations. He was on the wrong side now. A lawbreaker. To put it in terms of the old Westerns Mark watched alone as a child: he was one of the "bad guys" now. And he worked for even worse people—people that made "bad guys" seem like pretty good catches. Evil men. Heartless men who Mark was certain had no souls—not that they'd once had them and lost them along the way. Men who'd been born soulless and cruel and remorseless.

Of course Mark believed he no longer had a soul either, at least not one worth saving. He believed he had one to begin with. He'd never been a religious man, but he believed in God, and he figured that there were things God forgave, but he also believed there had to be a line, and that he'd very likely crossed it, if not by his own actions and deeds then by proxy of those for whom he hired out his pilot services.

Mark swathed his entire face and head with his forearm. The sweating was relentless, as if it came from a faucet. Down his face, underneath his clothing, all the way down into his boots. He *hated* the heat of Arizona; hated it so much that he'd promised himself a hundred times that the next person who said the words "dry heat" would get a shiv in the eye.

He stank. He'd not showered in three days because he'd not gotten out of *bed* in three days due to the stress from what was going down. Much worse than how he smelled, of course, was the person he had become. Most would call him a drug-runner. Or a money-runner. Mark wasn't sure there was really any difference and both might appear on the sheet of charges as they were read in a court of law. He didn't think there was really much of a distinction. One turned into the other and back again and Mark would fly whatever they wanted him to fly anyway, wherever they wanted him to fly it. It wasn't as if he had the courage to ask them something as bold as "what are you asking me to fly today?" and he certainly didn't have the balls to deny them, no matter what it happened to be.

Normally it was money. Mark flew millions of dollars of large bills north to Canada to be laundered and then back into the United States in smaller denominations and clean of all wrongdoing—from the accountant's perspective anyway. Mark of course knew the money represented a relentless flow of terrible narcotics into his own country (among others) and contributed to far worse crimes, a truly inconceivable amount of death and harm and addiction, even to children.

But he'd crossed the line in need of money.

Could the answer be so simple? Had he sold his soul for the almighty dollar? He and God both knew the answer to that one. Nearly all men sold their soul to that beast at some point. That was practically the *definition* of a career (though Mark didn't kid himself that what he'd succumbed to was far, far worse than drudging to a job he hated and dying without having accomplished the things he'd set out to do in life).

And the irony was that the young Mark Coulee *had* accomplished all he'd set out to do. And he had not done it with any sort of intent at all to end up a common criminal. He completed Aviation Officer Candidate School in Pensacola at the top of his squadron, served two tours in both Desert Storm and Operation Iraqi Freedom, made his twenty years for military retirement with distinction, accepted a coveted position as a pilot for a major airline— and he had *not* done all that with the intent to one day fly illegal goods for the Sustantivo drug cartel from the heat-baked desert of god-forsaken Arizona across the country and over the border into Canada.

Or had he? Was that the path that had always been laid before him and he just didn't know it? Could God be so cavalier and cruel? He wasn't even forty yet and his life had disintegrated before him as a dried leaf left too long in the arid heat. Laid off from the airline despite his unquestionably stellar record and reputation as a pilot— one of the best in their large-liner fleet, in fact—because seniority was all that mattered. While Captain Mark Coulee was risking his life overseas for his country, three-quarters of the pilots back home had gone straight from college into flight training programs and began racking up what would later amount to the coup de grace to excellent flyers like Mark:

Years on the job. Mark had never realized the seniority policy even existed until it sucker-punched him. Why would a company keep someone simply based on time and not skill?

After his layoff, his wife promptly left him. There were no other similar pilot prospects, not in the current economy, and Marla enjoyed the life of a pilot's wife too much: the steady money, the house they couldn't afford, the ability to spend what he earned while he was gone, her substantial time alone to choose carefully whom she would screw behind his back. Thank God they'd never had children; thank God Mark didn't have to worry about explaining his terrible plummeting from grace to *them* one day.

Oh, and Marla didn't just leave him either; she cleaned out the accounts. The house was already tits up, the Mercedes and Land Rover months behind in their lease payments, the credit cards run up to their limits.

Destitute. Him, a heralded naval aviator, a decorated war veteran, a hard-working, moral, successful man. Ruined. Pushed to the brink. Run down, run over, and nearly run into an early grave like his old man. For the first time in his life he really had no idea what his next move might be.

Until his best friend dialed him up on the phone. His best friend who flew for a different major carrier after leaving the military but had fallen out of contact with Mark over the past few years.

Samuel Jenkins.

Sammy.

Sammy talked Mark out of the bottle of scotch into which he'd lowered himself to dull reality and he did it quite easily, actually: by dangling an opportunity to make *real money*. A shitload. Fifty thousand dollars per flight.

Mark thought back on that night in the bar; the night Sammy came in, Mark already twelve fingers deep in whiskey, and talked him into throwing away any decency left in his soul for the promise of the big flow of green cash.

"You can't imagine how sweet this deal is," Sammy had said. Mark and Sammy had flown as pilot and copilot before, for almost ten years in the service of their country. They both retired at the same time from the Navy. Then Sammy eventually took another offer at a different airline.

Men who had fired rounds into columns of soldiers and watched them die horrible deaths in service of Country did not think about such things as *seniority at a commercial airline company*.

Mark wasn't an idiot, not even when he was so drunk he could barely keep his balance on a barstool. He knew nothing legitimate—nothing even in the *vicinity* of legitimate—paid that kind of cash. But he was beyond all that. Life had kidney-punched him once too often. God had deserted him long before. The next stop for Mark was to sell all his furniture, buy a sleeping bag and gas camping stove and squat in his own home until the sheriff forcibly evicted him and he set up camp under a bridge somewhere.

He had *nothing*.

And so there he sat; in that shitty little airport he'd flown in and out of so many times before. Sitting. Waiting. Sweating. Oh he had hundreds of thousands of dollars in foreign banks, but here he was, sweating like a bricklayer, the Cross of David in scorpion blood at his feet. Something had gone wrong, and it had been looming. Whispered looks. Rumors. Mark had just not known when, therefore the days on end in bed, showerless, prideless, and witless. And now it was late afternoon and instead of loading the plane with the money to be laundered north of the border, then waiting for the orange ball of fire in the sky to finally relinquish the day so they could fly the Cessna 172, blanketed in the obsidian darkness of night, Mark was waiting in an office with no air-conditioning; waiting for Cristóbal Casales, son of Enrique Casales. Father and son were two of the most feared men in all of Mexico and Central America, but the word had long ago spread through the ranks of Sustantivo was that Cristóbal redefined all the terms his father had established to put terror in the hearts of the strongest of men.

Mark was worried, not so much for himself, but for his friend. For Sammy. But his worry—like everything else in his life—was to be partitioned and doled out evenly. Today, Sammy received his share of Mark's worry; today Sammy was in the hot seat. His copilot—the man who had brought him into the fold and given him a fresh chance to rebuild his world financially. Best man at his now ruined marriage.

The rumors had been about Sammy. The cartel knew they had a rat. Some felt Sammy had been turned. Of course the gringos were suspected first, but Mark knew it could not be true—if for no other reason than he knew Sammy would *never* put at risk the money they were making. That was the whole point. That was *Sammy's* sell to *him*:

"We do our jobs," he told Mark that night, Mark stinking drunk and desperate for a way out—like the Ray Charles song. "Whatever is asked of us," Sammy told him, "we do. We don't make friends; we don't make enemies. We become part of the machinery. Then, one day, we'll break free. Until then, it's like any other job. You clock in, be the best, clock out."

So why would Sammy risk all of that? Had he been caught somehow? Had the DEA knocked on his door and told him that the Attorney General would be making only one deal and Sammy's name had come up? Turn on your lifelong friend and we'll hand you a cardboard Get Out Of Jail Free card? Still, how could he have done such a thing without Mark's knowledge? They flew every run together. Drank together. Degraded nice women in the bars together. They even worked out together at the same gym. He never saw it in Sammy's *eyes*. He would have seen it there; he was sure of it. Yet now, where was Sammy? In another room. Presumed guilty.

It felt as if a stone had dropped into Mark's bowels. If the cartel thought Sammy capable of such a thing—

Before he could deal with the stone in his guts, the door to the stifling office flew open and Cristóbal Casales burst into the room, larger than life, arms wide open, beckoning Mark out of his chair and into his loving embrace. Two men with mirrored sunglasses and necks like oak trees entered silently behind him, arms crossed, big gun bulges underneath their thousand dollar suits.

"Marcus, Marcus, Marcus," the younger Casales greeted him, patting him on the back heartily, hugging him hard as one would a brother, then grasped Mark's face with his huge, simian hands and stared him straight in the eyes.

"Cristóbal," Mark said, his voice shaking, betraying his deference to the man standing before him. Mark Coulee, who had held the rank of Captain in the Navy; the equivalent of Colonel in any of the other armed forces—he had been a Naval aviator and a war hero and Cristóbal Casales could, with a glance, have him pissing himself.

"Tóba," Cristóbal said. "I have told you, we are family, and my family all call me *Tóba*."

"Tóba," Mark said. "It's good to see you, sir."

"No, no, no—no 'sir'. Family, *tu eres hombre. Mi hombre. Mi familia.*"

Casales motioned for Mark to sit back in his chair and then wheeled over a second chair facing him. He sat, locking eyes with Mark once again. This time his expression had changed; a placid, unhappy look had washed away the moment before. His eyes were one color and not readable. Those were not the windows to anything, much less a soul.

"Do you know who is *not* family, Marcus?"

Mark didn't want to hear him say it. He knew the answer. He just didn't want the word to be spoken aloud. Maybe somehow if the name were never spoken it wouldn't be true. And even if it weren't true, if Cristóbal Casales said the name, it would *make it true*. Men like this; they did not take betrayal lightly. In fact such men loathed disloyalty more than any other thing in the world beyond theft of their profit (which was, of course, disloyalty itself).

No matter. Once the name was in the air, spoken by a man with the nature of a Cristóbal Casales, there would be no taking it back. When a soulless man spoke your name in irreverent, loathsome, accusatory terms, guilt and innocence became the things of children.

Mark shook his head and looked at the floor.

"Yes you do, Marcus. You know. I don't mean to imply that you *knew*. If you *knew*, oh, mi amigo, we would not be having this *conversación* right now. I want you to speak his name and then we are going into the other room and when we come out of that room, we will never utter it again, *¿Comprende?*"

"I-I understand, Cristó—Tóba. I understand," Mark said, shaking in his chair, sweating like a water buffalo, wanting to bawl like a fucking *baby*. "Please, let me talk to him. I know—"

Casales was shaking his head. "No, Marcus. It's well beyond that now. You know this. I would not be here. Do you think I would have come here, across the border, risking everything, if I knew this terrible thing not to be one hundred percent true?"

"This can't be real. This can't be happening."

Cristóbal cupped his hand behind Mark's neck and pulled him close. Mark could smell a mixture of tequila, cigar smoke, and breath mints. There was water in Cristóbal's eyes but Mark knew it was probably just sweat. "You think this is easy for me, *compadre*? He was my friend and employee before I knew you; family before you were family. Do you think I would act without, what's the word, *assurances*?"

Mark shook his head.

"What must be done *must* be done," Cristóbal said.

"Samuel," Mark whispered.

Cristóbal pulled him tighter, forehead to forehead, the power in his hands palpable. "Yes, Marcus. Samuel. My mother, she made the finest lechón in the world. That is all the suckling pig is good for, Marcus. For the slaughter."

He leaped from his chair, spun, and nodded to the gargantuan bodyguards as he walked past. They motioned to Mark to get up and follow, their faces void of any feeling, detached from any involvement beyond doing what needed to be done.

As he walked from the office Mark's knees gave way, he dropped, and vomited in a trashcan like a weak, terrified sorority boy who'd had too much to drink, sweat streaming down his face. As he stood, the two Latino gorillas waiting dispassionately for him, Mark Coulee felt the first tremolo of anger begin to quietly reverberate in his chest.

In the hangar four men in sweat-stained shirts hustled to load the plane—Mark's plane—with the bags of cash. Eight bags. The plane carried exactly eight bags with three point five million dollars per bag. Twenty-eight million dollars in ten thousand dollar packets. Not that Mark had ever looked at, much less touched one of the packets. But he knew. Twenty-eight million dollars crossed the northern border in large bills to return a few months later, laundered, with a fifteen percent fee absconded by agreement.

Cristóbal led the bodyguards through the room. The thick men in turn led Mark. They walked until they were at the doorway into another room in the rear of the building. It was darker and Mark's eyes took a moment to adjust from the dying sunlight that poured into the open hangar outside. But he could hear the soft whimpering of a child, or rather, the whimpering of a man whose spirit had been crushed beneath the omnipotent cruelty of other men until all feeling that had matured inside a man over a lifetime became childlike again.

Sammy was bound to a chair with rounds of dull silver tape, his clothing so red with blood there was no telling what color it had been before the beatings and the slicing and the clipping and the clubbing began. His head hung as if on ball bearings, the wires that held it upright long since snapped in two. He did not look up—could not. He was capable only of the low broken sounds, red bubbles of air forming on his lips, drool running freely from his toothless mouth. His eyes were purple mounds, swollen shut.

"The thing that bothers me most," said Cristóbal, "is that *he* went to *them*. Can you believe that? He wanted more money from us. He asked for *more*. I told him 'Marcus is the pilot; how can I give his copilot more money than him?' and do you know what he said to me, Marcus? *'Fuck him.'* I swear it's true on my mother's eyes. Greed. There is nothing more poisonous, more insidious, and more merciless than greed."

He walked behind Sammy, who had now stopped his whimpering and cocked his head as if listening, blindly wondering what would come next, perhaps praying for the sweet, adoring arrival of death. Cristóbal lowered his lips to one half of a bloody ear and spoke something between only them.

Sammy began crying softly, once again, the child, dreaming of a death that was too far away.

Cristóbal stood erect, straightened his suit, and motioned with his fingers as if calling someone to him. There was movement in the shadows and a dark-skinned man of Latino descent stepped forward, dressed in jeans, tan button-down shirt, and worn leather boots. His hands were crossed in front of him, like the gorillas that shadowed Cristóbal.

"This is Palo. He is your new copilot. Please, Marcus, make this your finest run yet. *Dios esté con vosotros.*"

Mark's head felt like a lead ball; he still could not understand why his friend would betray him. In betraying the cartel Sammy had done a stupid, stupid thing but had he thought at all about the fact that he was making the decision for the *both* of them? Mark entertained no fucking delusions; he knew he was lucky he was not back in the room with what remained of his friend. He also knew it was in part because of his own unmatched skills. Sammy would never be as good a pilot as Mark, and above all else, excepting loyalty, the Casales family respected employees who got things done and could be trusted with their goods.

The anger was no longer a simple tremolo inside but rather the kindling of a fire beginning to burn in his chest. Trust. Because Sammy had made *his* choice, trust was no longer on the table for Mark.

"I am sorry about your friend," Palo said in almost perfect English.

"If he's done what they say, then he's not my friend anymore. And you and I have barely met."

Palo held his hands up, palms flat against the air. "You are the boss, *jefe*," he said, emphasizing a thick accent on the last word only.

Mark stopped and turned to face him. "Do you have any idea how long that man in there and I have been friends? We were *soldiers* together. He is like a brother to me. And they are taking him apart in there."

"If what they claim he did is true, I would suggest he deserves that and more."

"My point is that you should keep your fucking mouth shut about my friend, or about anything else for that matter, and give me some time to process what the hell is happening."

"Si, Marcus. You're right. I apologize sincerely."

"And where did you come from all of a sudden? Out of the woodwork and, presto, another pilot? Cristóbal just had you sitting around waiting for a gig?"

"I was flying planes south, along the coastline of Central America—El Salvador, Honduras, Nicaragua—on my last run a Sandinista on a mountaintop got lucky with a burst from his AK-47. He chopped off my rudder plus a foot and a half off my right wing."

"And yet here you are? Alive?"

"I flew as long as I was able. The plane, she crashed in the jungle, but not until I was close to the Guatemalan border. I grew to adolescence in Guatemala. When I reached familiar territory, I put it down. I could not have gone much further anyway."

Mark nodded and started walking to the plane again. "I'm sorry to come off like an asshole. I thought I was going to die back there."

"I understand," Palo said.

"I feel like I should be doing something. Like I'm a coward for not speaking on behalf of my friend," Mark said.

"May I speak to you candidly?" Palo said.

"Please." Mark needed for someone else to speak anyway. He felt as if he were going to vomit again.

"The cartel can be very violent—their retaliation is cruel and without mercy. But they are not capricious. They do not give out such punishment as is being given in that room without being certain."

"It's not easy for me to say Sammy is no longer my friend," Mark said. "But under the assumption that he betrayed me—the cartel—in such a deceitful matter, I say it. Still I cannot wish for his death. That I cannot do. I still must maintain my humanity. At times it feels like the only thing I have remaining."

"I promise you, Marcus. Your friend back there— your ex-friend—he is going to wish for death before this night ends. He wishes for it already."

Mark stopped. "Stay here," he said to Palo and turned, heading back to the room where Sammy was being tortured. The gorillas at the door stopped him.

"Tell Cristóbal I need to speak with him. Tell him *now*."

One brute looked at the other and shrugged his shoulders. He went to get his boss.

"Marcus," Cristóbal said when he came out a few moments later, blood now on his own hands, his linen sleeves rolled up, sweat running freely down his face and neck. "Our business here is finished."

"I felt like a coward, Tóba. Not defending my friend in there. Not doing something to come to his aid."

"There is nothing more to be said about this matter, Marcus. There would be nothing you could have said to stop the inevitable. I told you we are certain and that is all that matters."

"But there is still something I can do," Mark said.

Cristóbal looked at him curiously. "And what is that?"

"I can beg you for his quick death. Clearly he has suffered greatly. The man in there was like a brother to me. I have served you well. I beg you, Tóba, to end his suffering now. Kill him. Do that for me, jefe."

Cristóbal stood there, as if contemplating all that Mark had just said. He then reached behind him and removed a 9 MM pistol from his belt. He pulled back the slide partway to verify a shell was chambered. He then held the weapon out in his palm, offering it to Mark.

"What I will do for you, Marcus, is allow you to end his suffering. If he were my brother, I would consider such an offering to be an honor. I honor you with this offer to deliver the mercy of quick death to our betrayer. To *your* betrayer, vato."

Mark accepted the pistol. A few minutes earlier he had felt drenched in the stink of his own cowardice. Now he was being offered an opportunity to be brave—not so much for himself but for the friend in the other room. Mark owed Sammy that much. He walked through the doors. Sammy was slumped in the chair again, bloodier, broken in more places. Mark crossed the room swiftly. He could not allow the bravado to drain from his will. He knelt beside his friend and whispered in his ear:

"I loved you, Sammy. I love you still. And because of that, I end this for you now."

Mark put the muzzle against Sammy's head and pulled the trigger, blowing a hole the size of a grapefruit out the other side of his ex-friend's skull.

On the way from the room he returned the weapon to Cristóbal and said nothing more.

Chapter 2

ON A clear night in the Wyoming sky there are so many stars that they begin to form in groups, as if some divine magnet were drawing them together. There is literally almost no room for any more. And the sky, it stretches literally from horizon to horizon—an enormous half-sphere full of the diamond sparkle of life and possibility.

It is spectacular, thought Sheriff James Pruett, *and I will never get over witnessing such majesty.*

Pruett found it difficult to have a front row view of the heavens and not believe there was someone or some*thing* out there—a rogue artist, perhaps—that had constructed the masterpiece called the Universe. The sheer magnitude alone was staggering and from his front porch he could see the light of stars that had died a billion years before, some at the time of the Big Bang. Pruett had witnessed such a star's death; its long deceased light would flicker and vanish.

Not unlike a man's life.

The old sheriff sipped from his iced tea with cane sugar and a splash of lime juice, closed his eyes, and thought of Bethy. The front porch was still a lonely place three years after her death. They'd talked their whole lives about building this dream home—talked specifically about the porch being the most important piece around which the rest of the house would be built; the long deck facing the mountains and showing the entirety of the northern sky. And of course they spoke of all the nights they planned to spend relaxing there, just as he was tonight. But together. Holding hands. The warmth of her love bleeding through her skin and into his veins.

They *did* get some of those nights in. Almost a year's worth before he lost her. Or before she was taken from him. But he'd been sober now for over two years. He and Jesse Claremont, after a few months of playing house, decided they made better friends. In fact, she became his sponsor and there were times he felt certain she was the meanest, hardest, least-forgiving sponsor he could have found.

This was a grand thing, actually—something for which he felt lucky. She'd kept him focused on what really mattered in life; kept him believing that no breath of air felt better or cleaner or more full of everything around you than one taken in the loving arms of sobriety.

Pruett looked over at Bethy's empty chair. The only other person to ever sit in it was his daughter Wendy.

I'm not sure I will ever find a woman worthy of sitting in your place, my love.

He wasn't sure he was meant to. And he wasn't looking. Fly-fishing filled in the summer gaps between shifts policing the town and then ice fishing filled those same gaps of time in the winter. He did them both alone. Him and whoever that bigger presence that sculpted the magnificence of the Universe. Pruett wasn't sure yet he'd figured out who that might be, or still just exactly what he believed, but he did know one thing:

If there was a God, there was no place closer to Him than Wind River, Wyoming and it was here that he would stay, make his decisions about such things, protecting what needed protecting, and live out the rest of his days. It had been that way with the Pruetts since before Wyoming was anything but a territory—James Pruett wasn't about to be the first to change that. His daughter lived a few hundred miles away but she was Wyoming through and through. He had little doubt she'd one day settle there, although fewer and fewer young people were staying put. Too many big city promises out there to entice them. Some left. Some came back. Pruett supposed that was the way of most small towns, not just his.

The sheriff thought back across the past several years since his wife was murdered. After the scene at the Townsley cabin the FBI and DOJ swept in and claimed immediate jurisdiction because of the federal agent that had died there.

It took a long while for the government to clean up their mess but Pruett had too much experience with *that* behemoth conglomeration to expect anything less. Bad publicity—particularly in an election year and with the economy in the crapper—was anathema to the government and any politician worth his or her salt. He knew exactly what they'd do. Gloss, shine, rinse, repeat. Pull all the evidence inwardly, offering up only what they had to— nothing damaging, nothing admitting any wrongdoing. They'd commence to licking their wounds then, applying salve where they could, healing externally as they went along, leaving nothing untoward for the public to see or to speculate about. A press conference here, a leaked report full of nothingness there.

Favorite newspapers, agencies, and reporters would always spin the story the correct direction and speed.

Just as the sheriff suspected, the official press release was vague and said only that a BLM agent had died in the crossfire of a land dispute in northern Wyoming and that there would be no charges because those guilty of the crime had been killed at the location by local law enforcement personnel. The Sublette County Sheriff's Department was commended for arriving on the scene and for containing what remained of the firefight albeit too late to save the agent.

Beyond that, few specifics were given, either publicly *or* to Pruett's local law enforcement personnel. Still, Pruett had a few friends in the government, and he made a call or two. Eventually a copy of a copy of an internal report was emailed to him from an anonymous account with a no-reply header. There wasn't much more in the feds' own report on the subject than he'd already seen in the papers or heard on the news.

The corrupt and murderous Agent Warren of the BLM received a full Senior Service government burial with honors. His stoic wife would have been handed a folded United States flag, a symbol of things her husband had long since thrown in the gutter along with his patriotism. It clawed at Pruett's conscience but he'd learned decades before that unless he was in the middle of true war, and under command, a man had a choice which battles to fight, and there were some that could not be won and, even if they could, would reopen dangerous wounds that had finally closed if not completely healed.

He took another drink of sweetened tea. Agent Warren. The snide, condescending, corrupt bastard. He'd gotten what he deserved, honorable burial be damned. Pruett neither knew where Warren had come from originally nor did he care. What he knew was the son of a bitch received Wyoming justice—a reckoning that was long overdue for a man who had been illegally bilking the state for years, maybe even decades.

Pruett's cell phone began playing a Faith Hill country song his daughter had programmed into it the last time she visited, interrupting the tranquility of silence and the opportunity of deep thought the old man so enjoyed.

"Pruett."

"Boss, this is Red Horse."

"Hell, Red Horse, I know your voice. What on earth is so important you need to call me now?" Pruett looked at his watch; it was only seven-thirty. After all that thinking it felt much later. "Go ahead, Deputy."

"Sorry, boss, I just got a call from Ned Lozier down in Stone Creek. Claims a plane flew overhead so close it took off three of the remaining four hairs on his head."

"At night?"

"Well, he sounded a little drunk…"

"Hell," Pruett said. "I'd only believe Lozier when he *was* drunk. He wouldn't know what to think if he was sober. He's the only man I know whose eyesight and other abilities truly do improve inversely with his sobriety."

"Yessir. Well, anyway, I called the airport," Baptiste said. "There ain't any flights in or out of there tonight. Not for several nights, in fact. And they've seen nothing on radar, which would of course validate Ned's accounting of events."

"Maybe some millionaire movie star outta Jackson," Pruett said. "Too busy showing off his pilot skills or making mojitos to pay attention to the altimeter."

"Gus at the airport checked with the tower in Jackson Hole. No small plane flight plans were logged at all today. And nothing big could be flying that low, not without shaking half the buildings in Stone Creek to the ground and not without every person in Wind River hearing it."

"Hmm," Pruett said. "Noted. No need for you to respond now, though. I'm guessing Ned Lozier losing a couple of hairs can wait 'til morning at least."

"Probably so. Sorry again, boss."

"Nah, don't be, Red Horse. You're the one working; I'm drinking tall, cool iced tea and staring into the stars."

"Roger that."

The sheriff closed his cell phone and took another pull on the lime sun tea. It was too strong. Pruett always made it too strong; Bethy had been the tea-maker in the household. But the flavor still reminded him of her and all things that reminded him of Bethy were good.

Pruett sipped again.

Most things, anyway.

"What the fuck is wrong with the plane?" Palo said just after he and Mark had unknowingly shaved the scalp of local rancher Ned Lozier.

"I can't tell yet," Mark said, lying to his copilot. There was nothing at all wrong with the plane. "She's sluggish. But the gauges look all right."

"Then bring it up off the top of the sagebrush," Palo said. "*Madre de Dios.*"

Mark smiled and pulled back a bit on the yoke, careful not to climb higher than the hills between them and the nearby Wind River airport. They did not need to pop up on local radar so close to reaching the mountains. Mark and Sammy had made this run seventeen times, though never exactly the way Mark would that night. They both planned to quit after twenty runs. One million dollars, in the bank, free of Uncle Sam's greedy paws. That was the plan, and there was no reason for Sammy to screw it up when they were *so fucking close.* A few more runs. And if Sammy had somehow gotten his ass in a ringer, he would have told Mark. They were best friends; they would have figured out the play together. And for that matter, why *hadn't* the feds come after Mark, too?

The flight up from Arizona had given Mark time to think about things. A lot of things. Of course Cristóbal didn't kill Mark, too. It was time for another money run and the cartel needed things to stay on schedule. To take Mark down at the same time as Sammy would put them severely behind and cost them far too many dollars. But what happened when they got back to Arizona? What were the chances of a hero's welcome? Cristóbal would never believe that Sammy acted alone. After all those runs—knowing the level of Mark and Sammy's friendship?

If Mark himself was aghast that Sammy could keep something like this from him, what would the *cartel* be thinking? Palo wasn't on this run as his copilot; Palo was his fucking *understudy*.

Learn the route, Cristóbal would probably have told him. *We deal with the other gringo traitor when you get back.*

What was the old saying?

Just because you're paranoid doesn't mean they aren't out to get you.

Mark Coulee did not want to die like that. Other than the money, he didn't have a hell of a lot to live for, that much was true, but he sure as hell didn't plan to die like *that*. Sammy was dead, at least. Mark knew approximately what Cristóbal would have whispered at the hangar in Sammy's ear that got him to whimpering again.

We keel you real slow, puta. I promise.

It was the cartel way. They were legendary for it. Keeping a man alive, on the brink of death, in unimaginable anguish, for hours. Sometimes *days*. And if Sustantivo—if the *Casales*—believed that Mark was part of the deal Sammy had made (and how could they think anything different?), that was the slow, agonizing death that awaited him upon return from this eighteenth and final run.

And there would be no one to speak up for Mark; there would be no defender to at least beg for mercy on his behalf, and without that, no one to end his life with a more merciful death. Not unless Tóba meant what he said about them being like brothers, Mark and he. Then perhaps he would receive a quick death. After all, for as much as the cartel touted their assurances, Mark himself knew for a fact he'd done nothing wrong, so if they killed him, he hardly deserved anything longer or more painful than a bullet to the brain.

It didn't matter. Mark didn't plan on dying at the hands of the cartel, either slowly *or* quickly. That was why for three hours he'd been silently sawing at Palo's seatbelt. A fraction of fabric at a time. Patiently. He really didn't have a plan beyond the now—he didn't think that well with death watching him so closely over the shoulder—but he knew he could not complete this trip with Palo at his side. Palo could never return to Sustantivo. Neither could Mark; but he also feared that even to finish this trip might be an egregious mistake. Palo could kill him in Canada just as easily as Arizona. In fact, the more Mark thought about it, the more it made sense that the cartel would view leaving Mark's body on Canadian soil—a case for the Canadian Mounties to solve—as the most desirable of outcomes. Palo could kill him, cut off his hands, steal his identification, and it would be *months* before the authorities would even be able to identify Mark much less pin him to a Mexican drug cartel.

So he kept the plane a little below three thousand feet until he was flying above the local lake, fourteen miles long, six hundred feet deep at its center. It was a small detour from the normal route but Palo would not know this and the lake was well protected by tall foothills on both sides and the Wind River Mountains to the north. Mark pushed the throttle back and said, "There's still something wrong. Can you see out your side? Does everything look all right? It feels heavy to the starboard side."

Palo twisted his body and craned his neck back to look along the plane's outer shell, back to the flaps, back to—

Mark rotated the plane ninety degrees clockwise, to the right side, and ran the blade of his knife through the last bit of Palo's seatbelt. Palo fell hard against the starboard door, trapped there like a man lying on the floor of a room, gravity pinning him there. The two men locked eyes for a moment and in that instant Palo saw Mark's desperate plan and showed—what—fear? Mark pushed down on the yoke and put the plane into a dive, then did three spins like he was dazzling the crowd at Miramar, throwing Palo's body as if it was nothing more than a bag of bones bouncing off the windshield, the roof, the seat, the door, but always keeping him and his groping hands away from Mark or the controls.

Over and over he pummeled the man, head against metal. Mark heard bones snap again and again; the interior of the plane was streaked with blood from the gashes all over Palo's head and arms and mutilated fingers.

Finally, when Mark was sure the man was either dead or unconscious, he ended the acrobatic flying and leveled the plane. Palo was slumped against the far door, his breathing labored, like a tired oxen demanding air. He was trying to speak but blood bubbled up from his insides. Mark set the plane on autopilot, removing his hands from the yoke, and leaned over, reaching for the door latch.

Palo grabbed one outstretched wrist, securing him in a surprisingly vise-like grip for his condition. With his free hand, Mark took the knife and plunged it into Palo's exposed ribcage and the man howled in pain, releasing the wrist-hold long enough for Mark to open the door. Freezing cold air came rushing in like a giant hand slapping them both across the face.

The cacophony inside the plane was deafening. Mark tilted the plane and gravity pulled Palo halfway out the opening, leaving him almost no handhold, yet still he tried desperately to say three indistinct words; desperate to make his voice heard above the wind swirling all around him, his breath almost gone, his life literally in balance over the glacier-fed lake two thousand feet below.

And then Mark heard what Palo was saying, over and over and over:

"D—E—A."

The small kindling of anger inside Mark Coulee that had first begun as a small tremolo burst into a raging forest fire, consuming what little was left of his innocence. *Palo* was an agent? Perhaps THE agent? Did that mean he'd turned Sammy? Or that Sammy was innocent and Palo was somehow part of the "assurances?" Mark stared into the pleading eyes of the man; Palo was barely hanging on. Mark's mind was running at full RPM. He just couldn't figure any other angle that played in his favor—Sammy was dead by his own hand, and Mark knew when he signed up for this duty he was crossing over a line; going to a place from which he and his conscience could never return.

"Fuck you," Mark said and gave a final shove with the sole of his boot. The man he only knew as Palo—Palo the DEA agent—tumbled out the open door, screaming in silence. And for a moment an updraft kept him right out there, floating for a few precious seconds next to the plane—like an angel, or a glider, or a bird.

And for that brief, heavenly moment it was as if man actually could fly.

Chapter 3

Three weeks later

DEPUTY MELODY Munney rapped lightly on the sheriff's office door but didn't wait for him to answer before opening it. "The hiker is out here, sir. Waiting for you. Tim Mackay, like you asked."

Pruett looked up from his paperwork. "Do you know the concept of the knock, Mel?"

"Sir?"

"You knock, you wait to hear something along the lines of 'come on in', and then you come in."

"I didn't think you were busy. Sorry about that."

Pruett smiled, waving her off to go and bring him the hiker. The one who had apparently discovered the tail of an undocumented plane near Sacajawea Peak.

The young man who walked into the sheriff's office barely looked old enough to be warming himself soup, had long, matted hair and a scraggly beard, and smelled as if he'd not showered in a fortnight. He wore a down jacket and multi-pocketed climbing shorts, wool socks, broken-in leather boots laced all the way to the top but untied.

"Have a seat—Tim, is it?"

The young man nodded. "Tim Mackay," he said.

"Can I have someone get you some coffee, water, a soda?"

"No, thank you."

"Are you sure? We aim to please here at the cop shop."

"Uh, sure, I mean, a Dew would be cool."

"It *would* be cool, Tim, but I think we've got cola, water, and the worst coffee anyone alive ever drank and stayed that way. Alive, I mean."

"Nothing," Mackay said. Edgy.

"Tough crowd, eh, Tim? No worries. This won't be anything *too* formal, at least not yet. Just some questions if that's okay with you?"

Tim nodded his assent. Pruett sized the man up. He had the look of someone that had to pee something fierce. "You need to use the restroom, son?"

"No, I swear, I'm fine. Can we get on with the questions?"

Pruett's smile slowly descended to a flat expression of disappointment. "You know, son, I have a daughter, probably ten years older than you. A lot closer to you in age than me, I'm saying. Then there's Deputy Munney. The looker who brought you in here. She's probably only four or five years older. You two go to high school together?"

"N-no. She was gone one year by the time I was a freshman."

"Point is, I've had some experience with young people your age. I probably look like your grandfather. Like some old relic time and the reaper just plain forgot to sow, is that it?"

"I don't know what you're talking about," Tim said.

Pruett wheeled his comfortable leather chair all the way across the office until it banged into Tim's outstretched legs.

"Ow."

The sheriff then leaned way out of his chair, until he was practically lying on Tim's chest, their faces about two inches apart. Pruett decided that Tim had missed the toothbrush for a few days, too.

"This is the office of the Sublette County Sheriff," Pruett barked like a drill instructor. "This is a law enforcement agency, Tim, and I am the man in charge of its running, that make sense to you?"

"Y-yes."

"It's 'sir' or it's 'Sheriff', Tim, and those are the only words I want to hear from you when you address me again, am I coming through the cloudy weather there, buddy?"

Tim sat up straight, pulled his legs in, and placed his hands on his thighs.

"Yes, sir. Sorry, Sheriff."

Pruett wheeled back across the office. "See, not so hard after all, is it?"

"Sheriff?"

"Showing a little fucking respect to an elder and law enforcement official, Tim. I realize your generation is a little crippled when it comes to such formalities, but I wanted to make sure we were on a level playing field before we continued."

"Yes, sir. I mean no—no, sir. Not hard. Sorry."

"You said that already, Tim. I'm not trying to be a hard ass. I'm going to ask you some pretty important questions. I just don't want you getting too bored or thinking I'm wasting your time. That's it. You give me a little time and respect and you can go back to whatever it was you were doing when Deputy Munney called. Capisce?"

"What?"

"Makes sense to you, brau?"

"Uh, yes, sir. Absolutely."

"So you were hiking, when, yesterday?"

"Uh, yeah. Well, climbing, sir. We-we'd hiked in, of course. But we were, uh, well, officially, rock climbing. On the spires."

"The Lady Spires," Pruett said.

"You know the area?"

"I know it surprises the shit outta your generation, Tim, but we were all young once."

Tim nodded but did not smile.

"Lighten up, Tim. We're good."

"Yessir."

"When did you spot the wreckage?"

"When I summited the middle spire—the highest—I could see the tail of the plane in the distance. At first, well, from a distance, I didn't know it was just the tail."

"But it was, correct? Just the tail, I mean."

"Yes. I'm—we're—pretty sure the front of the plane went down Solomon's Crevasse."

"Hang on," the sheriff said. "Let's not speculate. That's our job, Tim. You're doing fine just answering my questions. Can we stick with that for the time being?"

Tim nodded, fidgeting with the gray, tasseled stocking cap in his hands.

"The tail section, it was intact?"

"Pretty much," Tim said. "I mean, the, uh, wings or whatever, the small ones on the tail, they'd been torn off. But the main part—"

"The fuselage?"

"Yeah, the fuselage was intact."

"Who was climbing with you?"

"W-what?"

"Sorry to shift gears. I never asked before. You said *we*. Who was up there with you?"

"My girlfriend. Rachel. Just her."

"You two climb together a lot?"

"Oh yeah," he said, his face lighting up for the first time, glistening blue eyes widening. "We do all that stuff together."

"It's a good feeling, sharing space."

"Yes, sir. It is."

"Did she come in today, Tim?"

"What? No, I mean. No, sir. I thought I could tell you what we found."

"Well we like to hear both sides of the story."

"Sides?"

"Just an expression. Both accounts. You'd be surprised at what one person remembers and another forgets."

"Okay."

"You have a number where I can reach Rachel?"

Tim gave Pruett the number.

"So did you look inside the tail section," Pruett asked.

"Yeah, we checked it out pretty good."

"You went inside?"

"Yeah. Is that bad?"

"Not necessarily. Did you see anything at all? Out of the ordinary, I mean."

"Not really. No people, if that's what you're getting at."

"So just ordinary airplane stuff?"

"Yeah, I guess. It was pretty much empty."

"You waited to call until this morning," Pruett said.

"Sorry?"

"Well, you found the tail of the plane yesterday at, what, midday? You didn't call us until this morning."

"No cell service up there, Sheriff."

"Sure, sure, I know. But when you hiked down in the afternoon. I mean, even last night. I'm just wondering why you didn't call?"

"I guess I figured it was late and, uh, you know, best to get in touch in the morning, Sheriff."

"Makes sense," Pruett said.

"Yeah. Sorry. I mean, if you wanted me to call it in sooner."

"No, you've been a big help. Kind of a crappy way to end a climb. I appreciate you doing the right thing."

"The right thing?"

"Reporting it and all."

"Oh, yeah, of course. Glad to do it."

"Tim, can you go back out and wait where you were before? And send Deputy Munney back in?"

"I still have to wait? Uh, Sheriff sir."

"Just a bit longer. Promise."

Tim walked out and a few seconds later Melody came in, closing the door behind her. Pruett tore off a piece of paper and handed it to her. "That's the girlfriend's number. Rachel."

"I know her. My family does—Rachel Shepard."

"I want you to call her and pick her up for a statement. I'm going to have Tim write his down now."

"What's up?"

"They found something in that plane," Pruett said. "It's written on that kid's brow as if he worked on it with a Sharpie before driving over."

"I'll get him going on the statement and then find Rachel."

"Thanks, Mel. And keep it between us. As far as the young ones need to know, we're just gathering all the info we can get. Standard protocol; keep 'em separated; have Tim sketch out the location of the plane in relation to the Lady Spires. After he writes down his official statement."

"He told me he marked the spot with his GPS," Munney said.

"Have him draw it anyway."

Sheriff Pruett talked to Rachel Shepard an hour or so later, her boyfriend still working on his statement in an interrogation room. He found her to be much more stoic and certain of herself. Far less nervous. Still, she pretty much told the same story as her boyfriend: they were climbing the spires, Tim saw the wreckage first, it was empty, and they called in the morning because it didn't seem like waiting overnight would change anything.

There were no reports of any aircraft missing and Pruett could only think of the call a few weeks earlier by a drunken rancher complaining about a lone fly-over. It wasn't much to go on, but the two seemed at least even odds to be connected. And the sheriff was still convinced that Tim Mackay and Rachel Shepard found something in that plane.

After showing the two young climbers out, Pruett gathered his deputies—Red Horse Baptiste, Melody Munney, and Zach Canter—in the small conference room.

"Zach, I need you to go call Hal Porter over at the volunteer fire station and tell him we need the Search and Rescue helicopter ready to take us up there just as soon as he can do it. Go ahead."

Canter nodded and left the room.

"It's the opinion of our climbers that the front two thirds of this plane went down Solomon's Crevasse. If that's true, there aren't going to be any survivors and we're not likely to find much more than what those two kids claim they found. But Hal's both a pilot and an EMS and I want everyone in here to hope for the best and be prepared to treat survivors. Depending on how many went down in that plane, one man might not be able to treat them all."

"Those children," Red Horse Baptiste said, the Nez Perce coming through in his words. "They should have gotten word down right away."

"They're adults, Deputy, although young ones. No offense, Mel, but you've heard my speech on this before. It's the 'E' Generation. Entitled, Enshrouded, and Electronically Ensconced."

"Not all of us," Melody said.

"No, not all of you," said Pruett and laughed. "Not you. And I'd lay down cold hard cash that Rachel girl is *E for Enterprising.*"

Pruett spent the chopper ride to the mountains inside his own head, a place that could be comforting or terrifying, depending on who was running the reel-to-reel projector. It was too damn noisy to have any lasting conversation anyway. He couldn't stop thinking about the new generation. X or Y or E. It didn't matter what you called them; Pruett found them perplexing and nothing like his or any other generation he'd known.

He implied to Tim Mackay that Pruett himself spent time climbing in the mountains, and that was true, but not in the way this new breed of youth did things. Pruett and his friends hiked. They climbed when they *had to.* When *necessary* to reach the next objective. This new generation went in search of the next challenge. Then bigger and bigger ones.

And not simply rock-climbing. Hell, much of what they did made rock-climbing seem benign. Base-jumping; helicopter skiing out-of-bounds riding the front edge of an avalanche pouring down the sheer face of a mountain; and whatever that new sport was called with the winged suit that actually allowed a person to fly, if only for a few high-speed, life-threatening minutes. The death toll in that particular pastime was nearly fifty percent (and one hundred percent if one went at it long enough). Pruett had seen a special where a participant had lost three close friends inside a one month span. What was the damned *sense* in such sport? Forget the adrenaline rush—Pruett knew a lot of ways to plug into an adrenaline rush that weren't about to get him killed.

But things change, and so the minds of lawmen like Pruett had to be willing to change, too. How could you investigate a case without being mindful that the younger generation had gone insane?

The fact that many of the things Pruett and his generation did would have mortified his own parents was not lost on the sheriff, nor was the fact that now he was acting the role of old fart, shaking a disparaging finger at the youth of his own elderly world.

Still, Pruett swore there were big differences—gaping ones; differences as deep as the crevasses that populated the Wind River Range. You could compare them all you wanted but the old sheriff was pretty sure that any generation that required a bat suit and a leap off a perfectly solid three-thousand-foot mountaintop to find their fun had, at least, gone further than any before them.

"We'll put down there," Hal Porter said loudly, to be heard over the rotors and howling mountain winds. "On the Highline Trail."

They'd have to hike a bit to get to the spires, but nothing dangerous or technical. The worst would be the boulder field—an entire acre of rounded rocks, some the size of houses, where the crew would be forced to jump from rock to rock, brutalizing the balls of their feet despite the reinforced boots they wore.

When they finally reached the craggy rock near the Lady Spires, they had to circle the outcropping before they could see the white fuselage in the distance. It was at least another six hundred yards over rough terrain.

"A break," Pruett said, not meaning to sound as winded as he was.

"Old man," Melody Munney said and elbowed him in the ribs. "I guess 'E' must be for Energy, too."

"I'm twice your age, young lady. And still a better shot."

Munney smiled and Hal Porter sat down next to the sheriff. "I'm with the boss. At least long enough to catch our wind. This altitude can be a bear."

The rest of them nodded and picked a rock for their seat.

"Thanks," Pruett whispered to the pilot. He knew damn well Porter ran three marathons the previous year and was planning a trip to Hawaii one day for the forty-five and older division of the Iron Man.

"Least I could do," Porter said, and sipped from one of his UV-resistant water bottles. Pruett took out his own bottle and tried not to drink too fast.

When they'd rested ten minutes, Pruett stood stiffly. "Onward."

The group covered the distance to what was left of the plane fairly quickly. When they arrived they were unsurprised to find things mostly as the climbers had described them. The inside of the plane was bare bones.

"Where is Solomon's Crevasse?" Pruett said.

Porter pointed northwest. "Just over that rise. Not far."

Pruett looked skyward, back to the spires, and drew an invisible flight pattern across the top of the tallest outcropping, over the tail section, and to the rise where Porter had indicated.

"Debris field," Pruett said.

The rest of them squinted to focus in on the area between them and the hidden crevasse. There were bits of plane, what appeared to be a wing section, and probably more there they couldn't see. None of the group wanted it to be bodies; at least not dead ones.

Or pieces.

"I want to treat this tail section like a crime scene," Pruett said, motioning to the tailpiece. "Red Horse, break out the kit. Dust it all, bag any fibers, hairs, blue light for blood—you know the routine. I don't want to take any chances on what may have happened up here. The plane is likely registered to a dummy corporation or a non-existent pilot. This flight was never supposed to happen as far as any records are concerned; I doubt any identifying numbers we find will be legit, or at least traceable to anything or anyone useful, so this might come down to the luck of the Nez Perce and finding a fat thumbprint somewhere inside."

Deputy Baptiste nodded and took off his pack. "The Irish are lucky; we Nez Perce count on our cunning and skill."

"Just find me something and you can call it whatever you want. The rest of us are moving on to that debris field. I don't have to tell you what we might find."

The four spread in a skirmish line and walked at a slower pace, scanning around them. They wanted to be good detectives and not miss anything on the ground, but there wasn't one of them that was in any hurry to reach the wreckage ahead. Or the crevasse, for that matter. All of it lay out there before them, like a wraith in a nightmare, just beyond reach.

They found only wreckage along the flight line toward the main debris field. It looked to Pruett as if the pilot had not seen the tallest of the Lady Spires and had ripped the back third of the plane off—the sharp granite behind them would have sliced through the steel of the plane as if it were made of paper. The main debris field represented the distance the momentum of a crippled hull and whatever unspent lift existed under the wings would carry it before gravity did its job.

When they arrived at the scattering of plane wreckage, there were no people or body parts. Just insulation and loose gear, mostly, as if the plane had impacted on the rock rise ahead and all they were seeing was blowback of whatever had not been tied down. As they approached the rise that bordered Solomon's Crevasse, there was a massive scrape of white and pieces of exterior metal and a broken section of the right wing.

"The plane collided there," Porter said. "Clearly it was uncontrollable and yawing to its right when it hit the rise there. Ripped the wing—or what was left of it—clean off. And there's the propeller blade over there, far left."

Zach Canter put on his plastic forensics gloves and approached the right wing. "There's blood here, on the front edge of the wing and blown back across the top."

Pruett came over and examined the blood spatter. "Go find out how Baptiste is coming along. Get some good swabs of the blood. A spray like that—so far back on the wing?—doubtful that happened on impact," Pruett said.

Deputy Canter nodded and jogged off in the direction of the tail section.

Pruett walked slowly up the strangely smooth surface of the crevasse's rim. He'd been here once before, on a dare actually. The rest of the group he'd been with—most of them fifteen or sixteen—had been too afraid to walk up the rock for fear of what lay on the other side. The curvature of the rim gave the illusion one was about to walk off into space and the illusion was real enough that Pruett's previous experience did little to assuage the terror in his loins as he placed one foot in front of the other.

Upon reaching the apex of the rounded rise, Pruett found what he expected to find: nothing but a gargantuan hole in the earth that had no known bottom to it.

No plane.

No survivors.

No decent evidence.

The direction of paint scrapings, rock destruction, and tire skids left zero doubt as to where the rest of the plane had gone.

"Jesus," said Munney as she stepped up beside her boss.

The other two remained reverently silent.

Chapter 4

PRUETT WAITED for Malcolm Whitefeather in the Wrangler Cafe. The sheriff loved his staff—considered them more family than employees. They were each in their own way decent cops, too, but for some reason when he had what he thought of as "real detecting" to do, his first thought was to run what rattled around his head past his friend. Whitefeather had spent over twenty years in the Colorado Bureau of Investigations and had a procedural mind that rivaled any Pruett had ever known.

"Jimmy," Whitefeather said as he took off his straw Stetson and extended an aged, leathery hand to his friend.

"Mal, thanks for meeting me outside the normal schedule." Pruett shook Whitefeather's hand and the old Indian sat down.

"You kiddin'?" Whitefeather said. "This means you got something juicy, Jimmy-boy, and don't I know it?"

"I have some thoughts I want to run by you but first I have a strange question."

"All your questions are strange. And thanks for orderin' an old Indian a coffee before he got here all parched and whatnot." Whitefeather waved to the waitress and pointed to Pruett's cup, then executed a bunch of hand signals that were apparently supposed to clue her in to the fact that he wanted a cup, too.

"Last time I *did* order yours ahead of time and you told me that you didn't appreciate sitting down to lukewarm coffee," Pruett said.

"Yeah, I guess I did. What's your stupid question?"

"You seen any strange-looking people around town?"

"Shit, Jimmy, since the gas and oil companies came to town it's more uncommon to run into someone I *know.*"

"I'm talking *gut* strange—a worker from the oil patch or a gas company, they have a certain kind of look. I'm talking *strange.* Out of place, let's call it," Pruett said.

"And because I'm an Indian I'm supposed to be better at pickin' up on that kinda thing than the white man?"

"I was thinking more because you were CBI all those years you might have acquired some good instincts for that kind of thing."

"I was in the Bomb Squad, Jimmy. Now if there was a strange lookin' explosive walkin' up and down the street, I'd be your guy."

A second cup of steaming coffee arrived and Malcolm thanked the waitress and downed half the cup in one swallow.

"You through having fun at my expense?" Pruett said.

"Depends. Who's buyin'?"

"I got your coffee. We'll call it official business."

"That guy at the end of the counter up there," Whitefeather said. "Hard to imagine him in any regular routine around here."

Pruett waited a moment and glanced up at the counter. Sure enough, there was a Latino man in jeans, pointed boots, leather jacket, and sunglasses perched atop a mane of thick, onyx hair.

"See what I mean?" said Pruett.

"What I see is maybe I ought to be sheriff. What'd you do, walk right past him when you came in?"

"I've always said you were a funny old Injun. No, that spot was clear when I got here. Could be he's tailing me," Pruett thought aloud.

"All fun aside, Jimmy, tell me what's goin' on."

"You hear about the plane wreck up in the Winds?"

"Sure, most folks've heard one thing or another. No names were given, so I figured it wasn't anyone local."

"Not only that, the plane was registered to a pilot out of Tempe, Arizona. We're digging up the history on this guy but it appears he was an honest to God decorated war veteran. Strange he would use his own plane for mischief, you know?"

"And you're sure it was mischief, eh?"

"We also found blood on the exterior wing. Talked to a blood spatter expert in Cheyenne after I sent him pictures. He agrees the blood hit that wing at well over a hundred miles an hour. Up and over, in fact."

"Long ways for an unregistered flight, too," Malcolm said and sipped on his coffee, keeping one eye on the stranger at the counter.

"I never told you the flight was unregistered," Pruett said.

"Heap sorry, boss, me jumpin' to conclusions and all. They registerin' most flights bent on mischief these days, are they?"

Pruett smiled.

"You're right, no flight plan. Indications are he was flying low, too—probably trying to avoid local radar. That stretch of land between the Arizona desert and here can be pretty darn barren."

"You thinkin' drug runnin', then?"

"It's one theory that fits the profile."

"Nothing in the plane?"

Pruett thought he caught the Latino at the counter steal a glance back at them. "Looks like the front two thirds of the plane went down Solomon's Crevasse, along with everything in it. The tail section was empty. No useable prints; no nothing. Hal Porter flew us back and we got a bigger chopper to haul the tail and the bloody wing into town. The pieces are down at the County Shop in one of their bays."

"Whatever they were hauling they'd need better weight distribution," Malcolm said.

"Yep."

"Doesn't make much sense for the tail to be empty."

"No."

"Some hikers found the plane first, right?"

"Climbers they'd tell you. But yeah. Best we know they were first. Report of the low-flying plane came in almost three weeks prior."

"Some of those places in the mountains don't see human foot traffic for three years."

"This is a pretty popular climbing spot; not far from the Highline Trail."

"You talked to the climbers?"

"Yep. The young guy, Tim Mackay, he seemed wrong. Hard to get a warrant on 'seemed,' though."

"Hard to imagine anyone around these parts wanting to deal significant drug weight. Not exactly a hot spot for buyers, even were someone so inclined," Whitefeather said.

"There was a prime time news report a while back. Cartels doing their laundering north of the border in Canuck-land because of some new relaxing in banking regulations. That plane could've had a shitload of cash aboard, headed north."

"Cash is something everyone can use," Whitefeather agreed. "You know the ranger stations on both ends of the

Highline Trail have sign-ins. Most of the younger crowd don't like to use 'em, but those rangers up there keep a pretty close eye out."

"I had Zach run up yesterday to get copies for the last three weeks. There can be a lot of foot traffic this time of year; it's not a no-man's land like it used to be."

"You make a pretty decent sheriff after all. When did you interview this Mackay kid?"

"Couple days ago. I figure to let him stew and then bring him back in for a little bad cop, bad cop. Melody's been keeping an eye on him and his girlfriend, Rachel Shepard— she was with him up there. Nothing out of the ordinary so far."

"How can I help?" Malcolm said, waving for more coffee.

"I'm thinking of calling the feds."

"DEA?"

"Yeah. Wanted to know what you thought of that."

"Keep the government out of this as long as you can. Things turn south, I'd call the National Guard before the DEA. But that's just personal opinion."

"You worked with them on a lot of cases. FBI, I mean, but still the feds."

"Never trusted 'em," Whitefeather said. "I'd at least wait until you flesh this out a bit more."

"I keep thinking about those three weeks," Pruett said. "Plenty of time for the cartel to organize and beat feet up this way."

"And just like you, for all they know that money went down the crevasse with the rest of the plane. What're they going to do, burn down the town?"

"Famous last words. Think I'll move that watch on the climbers up to round the clock."

"Why's that?"

"Our friend at the counter just left," Pruett said.

"So?"

"He tipped his hat as he walked out the door."

Tim Mackay was watching a Warren Miller video when the knock came on his door. He considered just ignoring it but whoever it was knocked again.

"All right, hang on," he said, looking around for the remote that had been squeezed between two seat cushions.

He got up and opened the door.

"What's up?" he said to the stranger standing at the door. The man was tall—at least six-five—brown-skinned with tiny black hairs growing individually all over his arms and the back of his hands. He had a knife scar on his left cheek that ran from the bottom of his ear to the corner of his mouth.

"You should see the other guy," he said with a thick Spanish accent.

Tim smiled and the man gave him a half-smile back.

"I am looking for a young man named Tim."

"Tim. That's me."

"Then it appears I've come to the right place," the stranger said, looking past Tim and into the small one-bedroom house. "Is anyone else at home, Tim?"

"Uh, no, my girlfriend, she works."

"You no work?"

"What's this about?" Tim said.

"Money, Tim. This is about money, mi amigo." And the tall, scarred man pushed Tim on the chest and backed him into the house, pulling the door closed behind him.

"Hey, what the fuck, mister—"

The man balled up his fist and punched Tim so hard his jaw snapped and his whole world splashed crimson red and then faded quickly to black.

Tim awoke in his own bathroom, strapped with rounds of tight inner tubing to a board wide enough to hold him easily. The board was balanced with his head and shoulders on the edge of a full bathtub and the middle of the board on the stranger's knees as he sat on the closed toilet seat.

"I am Omar," said the needle-haired man.

Tim could not answer with a towel stuffed in his mouth.

"I think it is appropriate for the man who is to be tortured to know the name of his tormenter," Omar said and took a drag on the butt of a cigarette before putting it out against the side of the toilet tank.

Tim began to twist and turn, struggling madly to break free, but he could do little more than rock the board back and forth.

"Save your strength; save your strength, little man. You can look at it this way: tell me what I need to know, make me believe you, and you may walk out of here to do more of your snowboarding or whatever it is that excites you in life. Lie to me, and this is the last board you will ever feel, I promise you that."

Tim stopped struggling and looked at Omar intently, waiting to hear what would be asked of him. Omar shook his head slowly and smiled.

"First an example," he said. "To leave no doubt as to how serious a situation in which you've found yourself." Omar stood and lifted the middle of the board, dunking Tim's head and shoulders beneath the surface of the water.

Omar held the board in position while the boy struggled—five, ten, fifteen seconds—then sat down with the board, bringing Tim's drenched upper half out of the water. Omar reached down and pulled the wet towel out of Tim's mouth and the boy heaved for oxygen, spewing water from his lungs and throat.

"It's not like holding your breath at all, is it?" Omar said. "The towel serves to eliminate all possibility of doing anything but, well, *drowning*. That was fifteen seconds. It feels like fifteen minutes underneath the water's surface, no? I had this done to me—they put a piece of cellophane over my face with a hole punched over the mouth and poured water through the hole. Terrifying. Even for me—and I do not frighten easily, Tim."

Tim had lost control of his bladder—he could feel the warmness of the piss on his legs.

"Do not be embarrassed," Omar said. "No one—*no one*—can resist the fear. That is what makes this technique so much better than all the rest. Now I am going to ask you a question. You are going to pause, shall we say, five seconds before answering. I believe this is very important. People are programmed to shout out an answer in times of panic and terror. During these five seconds I want you to think about what being underwater for fifteen seconds felt like. I then want you to *imagine* what twenty-five would do to you."

Tim began to weep even before the question was asked. Clearly the imagining had already begun.

"Where are the bags from the plane, Tim?"

There was a silence of words in the room, the only sound the water dripping and tapping on the floor. After five seconds Tim said nothing, only cried harder.

"It's been five seconds," Omar said. "You may answer."

Tim shook his head. "The plane was empty—"

Omar stuffed the wet towel into Tim's mouth and put him under the water again. Five, ten, fifteen, twenty, twenty-five seconds. He waited an extra second or two before bringing him up and taking the soaked towel from his mouth. Tim was completely silent for a moment and then, somehow, with everything he had left, expelled the lungs that had nearly half-filled with water. Then he drew deep, gargantuan breaths, as if air were the only thing left in the world that mattered—not sex, not Rachel or his parents or his dog; and certainly not *anything* anyone could find on a plane.

"I waited a few seconds, Tim—a few seconds beyond twenty-five—and do you know why I did that?"

No answer—the boy was still too busy sucking in the precious air—and after only twice in the tub. Omar had put hardened men in the tub six, seven, even eight times. Of course they all died. They each told him what he wanted to know but he killed them for making his job harder than it should have to be.

Omar liked this boy. He wanted to hear the truth. He knew that what Tim told him this time was probably going to be the truth—he knew that by now Tim would give him *anything*—tell him all truths he knew in this world—just to keep the air and never have to breathe underwater again.

"I waited, Tim, because if by some miracle your brain had found a way to count, I wanted you to know that the air would never come as quickly as you wanted it to come back. Not ever."

Tim's breathing had returned almost to normal.

"I'll ask you again, Tim: where are the bags from the plane?"

"I swear on my mother's eyes," Tim managed, "the plane—was—empt—"

Back underwater he went. Omar did not put the towel in this time because this time he wanted Tim to see how long he could hold his breath; he wanted every second underwater to register in the boy's brain. He would feel the breath reflex begin to disagree with his brain—the brain would scream NO and the reflex would start to try and open, just a little, to see if maybe there was air out there, somewhere, even a little, and Tim would suppress it once or twice. But he would also know without a doubt there was soon coming a time he'd not be able to keep it closed—known as the *breath-hold breakpoint*, when the level of carbon dioxide had reached intolerable levels in the bloodstream—and Tim would involuntarily gasp for oxygen and breathe nothing but water.

The irony, Omar knew, is that once a human breathed in water, eventually the larynx closed the passageway to the lungs and filled the stomach with water instead (which was why so many near-drowning victims *threw up* more water than they expelled from their lungs). This phenomenon also led Medical Examiners to misread a homicide victim's state before entering the water, mistaking the small amount of liquid inside the lungs to mean the victim died before entering the water.

Omar waited until huge air bubbles rose to the surface and Tim started flailing and kicking and moving like he'd never done before and the board was tilted up again. This time Omar rolled the board on its side and punched the board right behind Tim's lungs and lower back with the heel of his hand—once, twice, three times—forcing the boy to vomit bathwater, as well as spew some from his lungs.

When Tim was breathing again, Omar placed him back in position on the tub.

"The next time you go into the water, Tim, you do not come out again. Not until the police come and pull your cold, waterlogged corpse from it. Do you understand?"

Tim just lay there, unable to move. As the torturer had seen so many times before, shock was beginning to take over. Omar needed to keep his victim's attention.

"You don't want to drown under the water, do you, Tim?"

The boy managed to shake his head slowly. No.

"Answer me one more time, then," Omar said. He paused for effect. "Where are the bags from the plane?"

Tim moved his eyes, swollen and so bloodshot-red Omar could not tell they were blue anymore—he moved them so he was looking straight into Omar's own deep brown eyes.

"Rachel," Tim whispered. "It was Rachel."

Omar stood one last time and looked down on his captive's broken countenance. "I believe you, Tim. There will be no more of the water for you, mi amigo."

Tim closed his eyes and smiled. The simple belief he would not go into the tub again was clearly enough for him.

The others—each of his previous targets—Omar had drowned. Sometimes it was because it was the easiest way to eliminate the subject, leaving the least amount of evidence. Other times it was because the target had confessed to stealing from the cartel and deserved such a horrifying end.

Tim was guilty of theft from the cartel even if unknowingly; even if by proxy. But Omar liked the boy. He reminded Omar of his son—this newer generation who did not pay attention to the old ways—who Omar loved dearly.

Omar removed the 9 MM pistol from its shoulder harness and before Tim opened his eyes once more, shot the boy twice in the heart. He could not put the child back into the terrifying water again. He should have; it is what he had done a hundred times before.

Still, he could not allow Tim to live. His oath to the cartel—his loyalty to *that* family—demanded that he kill one who had taken from the cartel, without hesitation. So Omar had chosen the only option possible: he left Tim such that the young man's mother could give him an honorable, open-casket funeral.

Chapter 5

"RACHEL SHEPARD just called 9-1-1," said Deputy Melody Munney. "Her boyfriend was shot. He's dead."

Pruett walked out of his office. "Tim Mackay was shot?"

"Says it looks like he was drowned, too."

"Christ. Red Horse, get Scoot and his wagon over there and gather the crime scene gear. Mel, you go right now and tape off that house. You comfort the girlfriend but don't forget for a minute she's still a person of interest. Scratch that, until we know what the fuck happened over there, she's suspect number one. Make sure she knows her rights."

Pruett's mind was already racing with thoughts and theories. Did the girlfriend kill him for his share in whatever they found in that plane? Was the stranger at the cafe really someone sent by the cartel or was Pruett letting his imagination run him like a track dog after the bone?

The one thing he did know beyond certainty was he didn't like murders in Wind River. The past few years had gotten them to "quiet town" again and he didn't want to see that change. Not now, not ever.

He went out to get in the Suburban, but there was a man standing in the shadows, just behind the truck, smoking a cigarette and leaning against the wood of the groundskeeper's shed. As Pruett approached the truck, the man put out his cigarette in the gravel and walked into the glow of the streetlight. It was the man from the Wrangler Cafe that morning.

Pruett placed his hand on his holster and the man put both hands in the air, lifted his leather jacket, and did a pirouette.

"I'm unarmed, Sheriff."

"Suppose you keep those hands where I can eyeball them just the same," Pruett said.

"Fair enough," the man said and walked closer.

He was older than he'd looked from a distance, skin wrinkled and acne-scarred. The bridge of his nose looked like it had been broken more than once and he had black, marble-colored eyes that sank way back inside his face, giving him a snake-like appearance. The eyes were mirthless and without a glint even into his soul—a soul, like the sheriff's, that had long ago been stamped as defective. The man stopped just short of Pruett's personal space and spoke in low tones.

"I've known men like you," the stranger said.

"That so?"

"You gringos have a saying. 'Big fish in a little pond.'"

"Been my experience you meet a lion on the Serengeti or in a nine-by-nine cage, he's going to maul you and clean you to the bone just the same," Pruett said, his face as expressionless as the dust at his feet. "Size of the fight inside, that's what counts."

"Is that what you are, Sheriff? A lion?"

"You have a name?" Pruett said.

"Yessir. I'm known as 'the man with no name'."

"In another life, another place, I would've kinda appreciated that."

"I introduce myself on special occasions only."

"Your name would be Death, then?"

"A smart man. Like you I have been that, too, more times than I prefer to count, but yes, if you learn my name, it's the last bit of information you take with you from this hellish earth."

"Quite a bravado," Pruett said.

"A tradition passed on by my mentor."

"Apparently his time of making introductions has also passed?"

"When he met me."

"Irony. I'm not immune to a little now and again, but I sense there are more important things you're here to discuss. So discuss 'em."

"Sheriff, have you heard the story of the man and the apple cart?"

"Enlighten me."

"It does not translate to English so well, but there was a man who had the best orchard in all of Mexico. His apples were so sweet to be legendary. But his orchard, it was a mile from the town where the vendors sell their goods, so he and his son built a beautiful apple cart big enough to transport his daily load to the market."

"Very industrious," said Pruett.

"Indeed. On the way to town the first day, a small group of very, very bad men, they stopped the apple grower. They asked him what reason there might be for them not to steal his entire cart of apples.

"The man said the only reason he could think of was that it would be wrong to steal apples and it would be right to let him pass. The bad men thought about this statement for a moment and then the leader said 'today, one apple for each of us. Tonight you and your son build a second cart. Beginning tomorrow, you bring two carts; one for us and one to take and sell at the market.'

"The old man, he pleaded. He told them that would use up his orchard of legendary apples twice as fast and make his profit half as much. The leader of the very, very bad men told him 'yes, but if tomorrow were to come and with it a great fire that burned your entire orchard, your house, and your family inside, you would then have *no* apples to sell at the market and no money with which to pay for the funerals.'"

"A sad tale," said Pruett.

"Not so sad," said the olive-skinned stranger. The pockmarks gathered like spiders when he smiled. "The apple grower was a smart man. He saw reality for what it was and he built the cart, his beautiful son by his side, his heavenly wife inside making apple pies to eat for after they had labored. He knew that the luxury of choice, it had eluded him that particular time."

"As far as I see it," Pruett said, reaching into his pocket for a can of snuff, "there's already one death in my town and I never even had the chance to build a second apple cart."

The stranger smiled even more broadly this time. "You are a smart man. If you help in the finding of all the missing apples, I will give you a hundred thousand carts."

"I'm not sure if I'm a smart man," Pruett said. "But I've dealt with your kind before. Speaking in terms of fish, you're one of those suckling fish that latch on to the *real* predator and survive off the scraps of bigger kills."

"I can't say yet whether you're a smart man after all, I suppose, but either way it would be wise to take care of whom you speak."

"I say what's on my mind. You'll find that's how most people in this particular pond do it. And I have no doubt that you are a very, very bad man, and that you speak for a larger group of very, very bad men. But I don't take kindly to threats. Never have. Once more you'll find most people in this area, they're the same. I also don't like talking in riddles."

Pruett packed his lower lip with tobacco and spit once on the ground, away from the stranger's pointed boots.

"Have you heard the word Sustantivo before, Sheriff?"

"Can't say I have," Pruett lied. "But my Spanish is limited to hello, goodbye, and 'where's the shitter, por favor?'."

"In my language we have many words for many things. And then there are the Columbians and the Nicaraguans and the Spaniards. To my people, Sustantivo, it means *the very best*. Not as you Americans think everything is best: Chevy, Ford, Dodge—all the best, no? Sustantivo has a special meaning. To be the best, you have to be willing to do what no one else will do, and there is only *one* Sustantivo."

"You know what? I *have* heard that name. It belongs to a drug cartel in Mexico, not too far south of the United States border. A cartel that assassinated a President, if I'm not mistaken."

"We do what no one else is willing to do."

"You do what no one else is stupid enough to do."

"You insult me yet again," said the man with no name. "When in Rome, I try to emulate the Romans, but it is challenging at times. I have a joke for you—I would tell you it is funnier without the translation but it's pretty funny anyway."

"I'm all ears."

"In our country lawmen serve only one useful purpose. Do you know what that is?"

"What's that?"

"Target practice," said the pockmarked man.

"You graced me with a story earlier," said Pruett, taking off his hat and wiping his brow. "Allow me to return the gesture. Do you know the story of the pioneers of the West?" Pruett said.

"Only from old Clint Eastwood movies," said the nameless Mexican.

"Yeah, those were mostly shot in Italy. Classic movies, not great history lessons. When the people that settled this place came out here there was nothing but animals intent on eating them, natives intent on killing them, weather intent on burying them—and every person who didn't come told them they were crazy. But they were not afraid. They were brave, even in the face of such terrible odds.

"Some died. Many. But the rest, they settled this patch of Wyoming. Most started in tents. And now their ancestors live here. Including me. You're going to find out that nothing comes easy here on this land, and you're going to discover that I serve those very people—the ones that elected me—and that I take orders from the law, not from the very, very bad men."

"One week," the stranger said, his scarred face a shadowed void of emotion. "If we do not have our money by then, I swear to you we will burn your precious little town down to a pile of ashes. That is no metaphor, cabron."

Pruett inched up to the man, close enough to smell the stink of his breath. "Others have made mistakes like you are right now, assuming because this is a small town, and that I am nothing more than a small town lawman, that I— we—could muster little resistance against you and your people."

"You have absolutely no idea about my people and what we are capable of, Sheriff."

"Have you heard of the honey badger?" Pruett said.

"No."

"Well the little bastard is no bigger than a fat house cat, but he's so goddamned mean there isn't an animal in God's kingdom that doesn't think three times before fucking around with him."

"Do you believe in God, Sheriff?"

"I believe in what's right."

"Well you, God, and your ferocious little honey badger better have our money back to us in one week, mijo, or all three of you will burn with this entire town of people you so valiantly serve."

Omar was of Peruvian/Hispanic descent and prided himself in his methods, but more than his technique and success—not unlike the surgeon—he considered himself professionally detached from his subjects. In the earlier days—when assigned his tasking by military supervisors—he'd had some difficulty, as many did, with particular subjects. He had the most trouble with younger subjects because Omar had a son of his own.

Over the years of service to the military he'd eventually taken to torture, finally discovering the peace of detachment. The subjects simply became inhuman to Omar; they were subjects, as to the surgeon people were patients.

But doctors considered their patients human and had sworn an oath to save lives. Omar had sworn his oath long ago to Sustantivo and the Casales family to professionally disregard life—old, young, male, female. He was an acquirer of valuable (and sometimes *invaluable*) information.

But he had made a terrible mistake with Tim Mackay. Tim was at the same age as Omar's own son—an unintended pregnancy with a woman to whom Omar no longer spoke. The emotional attachment to his subject had seeped back into his conscience without him realizing how dangerous such a breach through a crack in his bastion of disconnectedness could be.

He *did* believe Tim, but he had killed him far too quickly. He'd needed to acquire more specifics—and Tim would have given them—but now Omar understood how the suffering of this boy had connected to his emotions, finding the fractures in his stony heart where the love for his estranged son lived, causing Omar the Terrible to see his own child lying there, suffering, horrified, bloodshot eyes pleading for death.

And he killed the boy. Out of *compasión*—an emotion men in Omar's business could never afford.

Worse, he'd failed the cartel. Omar did not have anything to go on, more than Tim's admission that his girlfriend was involved, which meant of course that Tim knew more of the story.

Omar knew he could easily capture Rachel, and do the same things to her, but he felt as if something inside him had broken—like a small valve or cog or stanchion—something crucial in holding him together as the man hired to do what he did for a living. He honestly did not believe he could extract information from Rachel as—

An idea occurred to him. Rachel knew how her Tim had suffered. Perhaps simply the *threat* of such torment would be enough for her to give up the location of the money. Then Omar could succeed and go about either fixing this broken part or even retiring from such evil business.

He could go and find his son.

Pruett arrived at Tim Mackay's small house and met Deputy Munney outside on the front porch. Melody was talking to Rachel Shepard while trying to get the young girl to drink some hot tea.

The scene inside was not all that shocking to the sheriff; he'd seen torture firsthand. It left a scar on the soul, which made Pruett more concerned for his two younger deputies who likely hadn't considered that other people could operate in such cruel and psychotically ferocious ways.

The only thing out of the ordinary to Pruett was the fact that the torturer had used his weapon, killing the victim with two shots to his chest instead of simply finishing what he'd already started.

"Any brass?" Pruett asked Deputy Baptiste.

Baptiste shook his head. "The room is clean. No casings; no prints I can find; nothing but the victim's blood that soaked his shirt and ran down his sides to the floor below."

Pruett walked out to the front porch and sat beside the victim's girlfriend. "I need to ask you some questions, Rachel."

Rachel looked up with red, tear-stained eyes and nodded.

"Whoever did this, they were looking for something," Pruett said. "Looking *hard*."

"I don't know what," Rachel said.

"When I talked to Tim, he was giving me a nervous vibe. You both told us you found nothing in that plane. Are you sure you don't want to amend that statement?"

"He was acting nervous because he took the pilot's parachute. It was mounted in the tail section. He thought it was cool. That's it. Stupid, I know, but at the time it seemed innocent enough. I swear to you, Sheriff Pruett, there was *nothing else in that plane.*"

"I'm sorry for your loss, Rachel. Melody, she'll stay with you until your parents get here. I'd recommend staying with them for a couple days. You're still in shock."

"I don't believe her," Red Horse said to Pruett later, on the other side of the porch.

"Me, either," Pruett said. "Whoever did this to the boy showed some mercy. That means they believed him, though. And I can't get around the idea that if the answer had been that either of them stole from the cartel, there wouldn't have been any. Quick death, I mean."

"The boy, he endured very much pain before he died. Inside I saw no mercy," Red Horse said.

"Maybe not."

Baptiste thought for a moment. "If someone did find anything in that plane, that's fifteen miles in *and* out, from either side. And cargo so large as to warrant a plane to fly it around is not something you just throw in your backpack."

"Horses," Pruett said. "Someone would have had to bring in horses."

"Yep. Either they were already up there with 'em or they brought some in, after the fact. Could have hid the stash up there pretty easy. Come down and gotten horses."

"They'd have to rent them. Couldn't bring any outfitters up. How would they explain the boon?"

"Not many outfitters are willing to rent their horses without them coming along on the ride," Baptiste said. "Not good horses, anyway."

"We start with Zach's list. Anyone who takes horses into the wilderness is required by law to have a permit *and* to sign in and out. And the rangers do a cursory inspection of the animals in both directions to cut down on poaching. If someone took animals into the wilderness to pack out what was on that plane, there will be some kind of a record of it. And a ranger may have noticed something out of the ordinary."

Rachel had just left the post office in town the day after her boyfriend's murder when Omar seized her, immobilizing her with a short-acting toxin delivered through a needle into her neck and sweeping her limp body into the back of his van without anyone noticing a thing.

At this he was still the expert.

Omar took the girl to a remote place—an unused cabin in the woods he'd found earlier that was miles from anyone, just in case Rachel tried to scream (or he found his old knack again).

His captive woke up in a chair bound in duct tape and gagged. Omar sat facing her in a replicate chair, as if he'd been waiting patiently for her to reawaken to reality.

"We're a long, long way from anyone hearing you, and though I've grown accustomed to every manner of screaming, pleading, begging, and howling imaginable, I am a tired man today. If I remove your gag and allow you some comfort will you chat with me and promise not to shout or scream?"

Rachel nodded.

Omar gently untied the gag and removed it from Rachel's mouth.

"Why did you take me?" she said, still groggy from the drug.

"Now, Rachel—if this is how we are to begin, how do you think this conversation is going to end? I gave Tim the opportunity to simply talk and tell the truth. You found him, I assume. Let's not play games and end up at the same point."

"You fucker," she said. "You killed the man I love."

"Hmm," said Omar. "The man you loved more than the money?"

"What's that supposed to mean?" she said, tears on the cliffs of her eyes but falling nowhere.

"I am going to make you a promise, pretty lady. If you tell me everything, and it matches what Tim told me, I will not torture you. You will never have to endure what your boyfriend suffered. If you lie to me, even once—even the smallest fib—not only will you endure that, you will find out just how pretty I think you are."

"Pig," she spat.

Omar's eyebrows raised and his mouth became an impish curve. "Perhaps. All I want, however, is to know if we have a deal?"

Rachel looked at her feet, no doubt picturing Tim the last time she viewed him, Omar thought.

"Yes."

"Who found the money?" Omar said, and leaned back comfortably, missing his pipe at home and glad he might not have to hurt this young woman.

"I did."

"Tim?"

"Tim was still back at the spires. I saw the plane; I wanted to find out what was in it."

"First," Omar said.

"What?"

"You wanted to find out *first.*"

"Yes."

"And what did you find in the plane?"

"Seven black duffel bags full of money."

Omar paused. "I was clear with you before; about the truth?"

"Yes."

"What did you do next?" Omar said.

Rachel's cheeks pooled with color; arterial red.

"I moved the bags. I hid them behind a nearby rock formation."

"And then you told Tim?"

"No."

"No *what?*" He wanted to hear her say it.

"I never told Tim about the money."

"Not ever?"

"Never. You killed the wrong man," she said.

"Wrong person. *I killed the wrong person* is what you meant to say. The less greedy one. The less competitive one. The less selfish one. *The less conniving one.*" With each syllable Omar spoke his voice raised a decibel or two in volume; gained more surety. The torturer inside, alive for so many years and sleeping but only a day or so was awakening inside him.

Tim. He had liked Tim.

"Do you know he protected you until the very last? He knew something—more, perhaps, than you knew—but he loved you enough to endure Hell before saying your name."

"I'm sorry," Rachel said, trying to produce a modicum of sincerity that never rose above a fearful squeak of anxious self-preservation.

"Did you retrieve the money?" Omar said, nearly whispering.

"No."

Omar stood, grabbed Rachel by her long, silken hair and dragged her, chair and all, into the bedroom.

He didn't bother with the gag. He preferred a woman who made her pleasures and pains known to her man.

Back at the station Pruett sat down at Deputy Zach Canter's desk. "Talk to me."

"A pretty long list of people going in and out," Canter said. "But I narrowed it down to anyone with horses, like you asked. Since it's not hunting season, there are only four documented entries on horseback for the three-week period."

"That's not bad," said Pruett.

"One was a Boy Scout troop that hired Jensen Outfitters to take them up for a week-long camp. I'm thinking we can set that one aside for now."

Pruett smiled. "Agreed."

"Of the other three, two are actual businesses—Morgan Outfitters and the Circle B—the third is a pair of locals who appear to have rented their mounts. Keil Shriver and Frank Purdy. The brand on the horses was the Black Jack Ranch up near Flat Top Mountain."

"The Beard brothers," Pruett said. "Shriver is kin to them. Cousin, I think."

"Neighbors of yours, ain't they?"

"Some of their land butts up against some of mine. Wouldn't call them neighbors; the Beard brothers aren't the neighborly type. More criminally enterprising than mountain outfitting, as you know."

"Sounds like a starting place to me," Canter said. "I could go up and ask some questions—"

"You're a good cop, Zachary. But I've dealt with the Beards before. You poke around the other two outfitters, see what their charters were, who they took up, etcetera."

"I can handle myself, boss."

"I know you can, Zach. Like you said, they're my neighbors, and though we're not friends, I have a rapport with 'em. That's all it is, son."

"Okay."

"'Sides, I have to be honest with you: the Beard brothers? Not sure how those two could get up into the Winds, much less find anything. Shitty cowboys and inept marijuana growers, they are. Unsavory and violent as hell if you meet 'em drunk somewhere in a bar? Yes. Criminal masterminds? I'm voting no on that ballot."

"You can't seem to find those elusive, ineptly grown plants," Zach said, smiling.

"Ouch. Touché, my charge. Touché."

Pruett gave Malcolm Whitefeather a call but it went to voicemail.

"Hope you know how to leave a message cuz I ain't able to tell you. Bye."

And then a few seconds of Whitefeather grumbling, trying to figure out how to end his recording. Finally, a beep.

"Mal, give me a callback as soon as you get this message."

He started driving north, toward Flat Top, his place, and the Black Jack Ranch. The Beards truly were a surly crew. They were not evil men but were not classical ranchers either. They'd been formally charged with cattle thievery that the State was unsuccessful proving in a court of law but Pruett had been convinced for years that their illegal enterprising went deeper than that. In point of fact, he knew it. Just as they knew the Beard brothers—Val and Tom—had stolen the twelve head of Angus of which they were accused, Pruett knew they made (and sold) some other illegal earth-grown products, but they were rascally bastards that made it difficult to pin much on them other than being the most disagreeable, unsavory bunch he'd met.

The sheriff's cell phone started singing at him again and he silently swore he'd figure how to change the damn thing over to a respectable phone-sounding ring. The caller ID said M. Whitefeather.

"Mal," Pruett said.

"Is that what passes for a proper answer of a phone these days?" said Whitefeather.

"I'm on my way to the Black Jack Ranch. Looks like a cousin of the Beards may have borrowed or rented some horses and taken 'em into the Winds during our alleged timeframe."

"Shit. You want me to get in the truck and come up, too?"

"No," said Pruett. "But if I don't come back, I want you to avenge me."

"Now who's the funny guy?"

"I had a visit from our friend at the diner," Pruett said.

"He step on your toes?"

"Just a little. Said they'd burn our town down to the ground if we didn't have their money to them in a week."

"Did this guy grow up watching Italian Westerns?" Whitefeather said.

"I don't think he was kidding, Mal."

"He and his pals are gonna find out about what kind of resolve we have in these parts."

"That's what I told him."

"How much time before doomsday?"

"The week's up come Friday. Six more days."

"You figure the Beards are involved?"

"Not necessarily. Not if I was a betting man, I guess," Pruett said.

"Good thing you're more the drinkin' sort."

"Is that what passes for 'funny' these days?"

"Sorry. My sense of humor in old age does about as well as my plumbing. Gettin' old sucks, even for an Injun. I've got a better idea. You turn around, come out to my place instead. Let's drink some of my special Blackfoot sweet tea and discuss a real plan—one that doesn't involve you goin' out to the Beard place by yourself. Them sad excuses are tough and mean."

"Which means I'm not?"

"Which means two against two is better odds, you old fart."

"I'll come by after," Pruett said. "I want to check them off the list, that's all."

"Don't give me that shit and tell me the sun's shinin'. You'd take any excuse to rattle the cage of those racist bastards and you know it."

"I'm not saying I won't take some pleasure in it, but we're neighbors. I'll be okay."

"Shit, I suppose there's no way you'd pull over at the Willow Saloon and drink a hot coffee until I can drive out and back you up."

"Already past there, Mal. I'll be all right. You'd be surprised at how much better I've got at this sheriffing thing since we spoke last."

"You're a fucking helluva sheriff, Jimmy. You leave the stick for poking in your car and when rattlin' cages, keep your fingers on the outside."

The drive up to the Black Jack began as did Pruett's drive home each evening. The gravel road was flat and smooth until about three miles in, where state maintenance ended, and then it became more of a four-wheel drive path that bounced a vehicle right, left, up, down, and was not for the weak of stomach. A mile and a half on the shitty county road and there was a fork: right went on and eventually got you to Pruett's property; left went toward Flat Top Mountain and circled up behind Pruett's place. The turn-in to the Black Jack Ranch was another half mile in.

Pruett drove up past the corrals of mountain-bred horses and stopped by the gaggle of vehicles, some in various states of disrepair, at the main house. He got out of the Suburban and was met by Val Beard, the older of the two brothers who ran the ranch.

"Sheriff," Val said and touched the brim of his hat.

"Val, it's been a while. Good to see you."

"Wish I could say the same. Sheriff don't normally come a callin' less there's a lawful need."

"Just a couple questions is all," Pruett said. "If I'm not interrupting."

"Nah, always got time for a neighbor. Even when he's dropped in as Sheriff. Come inside and we'll sit."

At the kitchen table Beard offered him a whiskey and a beer.

"Been dry two years now," Pruett said.

"Damn. Well, shit, I don't know the rulebook, Sheriff. Can a drunk drink his whiskey in front of an ex-drunk or is that bad etiquette?"

"Drink your whiskey," Pruett said, trying to be unaffected, but the animal in his belly stirred, as if it had just woken from slumber. And the animal was always thirsty.

Val Beard threw down a shot and took a sip of the cold beer. "What kinda questions you got?"

"You rent a couple of horses a little while back to Keil Shriver and Frank Purdy?"

"Nope," Beard said and poured a second whiskey. He downed it before continuing. "Loaned 'em. Don't take money from kin, long as they're half a horseman."

"Any thoughts on what they were doing up there in the mountains?" Pruett could smell the whiskey from across the table. Soon the animal would have him sweating. He wanted to be gone before he showed his weakness like that.

"Got me lots a thoughts," Beard said. "Who knows? Cousin Kiel's half queer anyway; maybe they was goin' broke-back on the mountain."

"They have anything with them when they came back down?"

"You sure you don't want a sip?" The cowpoke threw back a third whiskey and then swallowed half the beer. "Mm, goddamn, Sheriff, my hat's off to ya. Life without a little whiskey sure seems like a tough one to me."

"The boys, they bring anything down with 'em you know of?"

"Nothin' but maybe some used condoms in their saddlebags. I don't frisk kin neither. Queer or not. No offense."

"What the fuck you mean by that?" Pruett said. The animal would soon have full control of his temper, too.

"Oh not that you're queer, Sheriff. Hell no. You're a man's man through and through. I just meant, you know, no offense to skin color or nothin' like that." Pruett could see the whiskey reaching Val's person, warming him up, making him a hair meaner, eyes starting to burn with that fire.

"Man pokes fun at gay men, he's a bigot," Pruett said. "Not a racist."

"Right, I always get the two confused."

"So officially you don't know of anything came down from those mountains, Val. Is that what I should be writing down?"

"If your memory requires it."

"Nothing."

"Nope. Not a goddamned thing."

"Keil, is he here at the ranch?"

"Nope. At his place in town, I would guess."

"Obliged for your time, Val. Enjoy your drinks. I'll let myself out."

Beard followed him to the door. "Watch them potholes on the way out, Sheriff."

Pruett wiped a sheen of sweat from his forehead. The whiskey—so close; so salaciously tempting—had unbalanced him. He was an alcoholic; booze would always be his weakness, but to show his cards like that in an interview was unacceptable. He'd come farther than that.

And now he wanted a fucking drink more than anything. So much he'd go back and have one with that racist bastard Val Beard. That's how little the animal catered to a man's self-respect.

Pruett called Jesse.

"Hello, James. Are you all right?"

"No. I'm a click away, Jess. Thirsty as a drunk gets."

"Come on over. I'll make some fresh coffee and we'll talk it through."

"I'm sweating like a beast."

"Come over and you don't stop until you get here."

When Omar was finished with the girl he left her tied to the bed, gagged, bleeding, and weeping. The cabin was a long way from any listening ears but he needed to follow up on what pillow talk she'd been willing to give up. He left her alive because he knew—feared, actually, as the beast of his earlier decades had not fully returned and he still wanted to quit this business and find his son—there was still a chance he would need more information from her, and he needed her alive to get such information. He would not fail the cartel, particularly if this were to be his final job.

Rachel had not gone to get the money herself. She believed it to still be where she hid it. But she had mentioned finding something to a friend—a man with whom she'd been cheating on her beloved Tim—a man named Skylar Durden.

Omar was on his way to Durden's house in town. It was dark by then. It was going to get darker for this young man if Omar didn't hear what he wanted to hear. He was tiring quickly of this business. He was not a private investigator or detective. He was moving beyond his *especialización.*

Omar approached Durden's small house and turned off his headlights, parking a few doors down on the asphalt street. A nice, quiet neighborhood. He exited the car and stayed in the shadows. A few lights were on at Durden's dwelling so Omar did some reconnaissance. He looked in a few side windows, went into the back yard and peered through the sliding glass door from the cement slab patio. He tried the door and found it unlatched. Omar had already seen Durden in his living room reading a magazine.

By the time Durden saw Omar's face, it was too late to avoid the fist that smashed the cartilage of his nose and practically knocked him out right there on the couch where a moment ago he'd been nearly dozing off to sleep. Omar stuffed a small towel in Skylar Durden's mouth and then sat atop his chest as if he were riding a bucking bull in the rodeo, only the boy beneath him seemed small and underfed and was easily held motionless and without much breath by Omar's tall, muscular physique.

When he finally had Durden's attention, the boy's brown eyes locked with his own, Omar spoke softly, so as not to be detected by anyone in a neighboring home. "Do you think it is an acceptable thing, sleeping with another man's woman?"

Durden could not speak through the gag but shook his head emphatically *no*. Blood from his damaged nose was beginning to soak the towel in his mouth, cutting off even more of the air to his lungs. His eyes were also watering, both a side effect of the blow to his nose and likely a fair amount of momentous fear.

"Yet you fuck Rachel Shepard behind the back of your dead friend, Tim. I do not understand such contradictions. By the way, allow me to introduce myself: I am the man who tortured and killed Tim. Oh, and I fucked your Rachel, too. So you'll know that. I hope it hurts you. I hope it pains you to know that in the end she gave herself up to me and anything that I wanted, boy."

Durden closed his eyes and began to utter strange sounds, almost like those of the un-whelped puppy: squealing softly, innocently, not capable of understanding anything around them or of what came next.

"So that you know, Mr. Durden. I liked Tim. Quite a lot. And you can imagine my disappointment when I discovered from Rachel—who by the way is currently going nowhere but is recovering from what might be considered a quite brutal yet satisfying session in bed—that Tim knew nothing of the money that his girlfriend—the one you were fucking behind his back—found. I have my own guess as to how the plans were laid between you and Rachel. All that money. Two love-struck young people, travelling the world, perhaps? Or were you stupidly going to stay here? Build a magnificent house everyone in town—and the IRS—would know you could not afford. Did you think at all? That someone out there in the whole wide world might be missing twenty odd million dollars? Ah, of course you didn't. Men with so little loyalty to their friends that they allow their dicks to lead them around in life aren't smart enough to consider a few, much less many, incongruous angles. I can only assume you are quite the lover, Mr. Durden, since poor Tim could not keep his girlfriend from your wiles. At least in this short and pitiful life you may have had *that*."

Durden opened his eyes, filled now with terror instead of water. He shook his head 'no' again, but this time without conviction; this time he maintained only the feebleness of one who has realized there is only despondency in his future and the level of pain, pleasure, or even the amount of air he would be allowed to breathe, rested completely at the discretion of a madman.

Chapter 6

WENDY STEELE finished her run around the streets of downtown Laramie, the air dense with pleasant moisture and the normally unnoticed odor of the cattle yards miles outside of town. Even though most residents lauded the fact that *you got used to the smell*, that scent would always conjure images of home—of Wind River. The loamy, leathery, fecund odor of Angus and Hereford and Longhorns.

She walked the deserted streets, cooling down, enjoying the embracing joy of solitude. She'd been thinking about home a lot lately, particularly about her father. She'd changed her name so long ago out of wrath. She wanted to show her dad that they truly had mended fences and reconnected (though she knew he already felt the love that had been exploding from within each of them since her mother had died). She figured if she changed her name back to Wendy Pruett, it would perhaps be a symbol only, but a heartfelt one—and symbols were not all just kindling wood for the starting of a blaze; they were important, too.

The flag of a country.

A wedding band.

A pink ribbon.

Human beings had an embryonic need for things to see, touch, feel, understand, and warm them when the decent thoughts had retreated and a heart needed a grappling hook or at least a reasonable handhold before it let loose and fell into the obsidian unknown below.

Wendy knew her father's heart needed handholds more than ever, particularly after losing his best friend and companion of forty-plus years. His rock. His better half (and *that* she had been, for many years). Wendy hoped that changing her surname back to her father's with a love equal to the anger she felt so many years ago would give him one. And if she were being honest it would assuage a guilt that had festered inside her soul for far too long.

The loft above the Buckskin Bar she shared with her lover, J.W. Hanson, Professor of Law at the University, was still a few blocks away. She'd been pondering her reverse-cougar lust for an older man—a father figure? Either way, the affair had turned into full-blown love. There *was* a sizable difference. Jay was twenty-eight years her elder.

Bullshit—she hated the word "elder" almost as much as she hated thinking in clichés. He was older than she was. Not some cutesy "fifty-seven years young." He was fifty-seven. Humans aged, and when they did—all of them— they died. Human beings aged every day of their lives—not only Jay—her, too. And yes, the process did accelerate the older one got, but Wendy *wanted* to take care of the man she loved—not just in old age but now. Always. Good times and bad. That was what love meant to her.

Most people didn't consider old age until it had crept up on them like a thief in the night; but not Jay. J.W. Hanson was, after all, one of the finest defense attorneys to have practiced law. He thought of such things far in advance.

Lawyers were trained to be two things above all else: thinkers and realists. Each situation in an attorney's career—particularly for the criminal defense attorney— depended on the ferreting of every eventual scenario and, sometimes most importantly, the ability to find the weak spots in the law and also the moments when the law could be bent nearest the breaking point for a client.

No one taught this, of course (at least not in any textbook)—at school, the Law lorded over all as a dictator over those he repressed. But becoming a lawyer was about thinking of all the possibilities. Every angle. What their opponent would plan as a strategy and when they would execute each element so that being a step ahead became second nature. Just as the best warriors knew what their opponents would be thinking before *they* did.

In his staff office Jay had a quote mounted on a plaque. It occupied one wall and the other wall featured his aged Sun Tzu quote—the Tzu quote had been the only thing to adorn his law office walls for his decades in the courtroom. An author Jay had never read before he'd heard the quote penned the new mantra. Robert Jordan (a pen name for James Oliver Rigney, Jr.—a highly decorated Vietnam war vet and monumental hero) wrote in his book, *Crossroads of Twilight*:

"If your enemy offers you two targets, strike at a third."

J.W. Hanson *the attorney* felt it quantified his "know the mind of your opponent" maxim even more summarily than his previous dictum ("If ignorant both of your enemy and yourself, you are certain to be in peril.")

Wendy, less warlike, preferred Marcus Aurelius:

"Live a good life. If there are gods and they are just, then they will not care how devout you have been, but will welcome you based on the virtues you have lived by. If there are gods, but unjust, then you should not want to worship them. If there are no gods, then you will be gone, but will have lived a noble life that will live on in the memories of your loved ones."

It was long but it also covered her (and her father's) innate indecision about God and all the rest. The problem was, neither that quote nor any of her own had solved her immediate questioning of the future of her and her lover.

How much pain would she put *him* through on top of whatever anguish came calling each new year into senior citizenship? The more he suffered, the more she would live to help him and the more she helped him the more aggravated he would become. It was her first unsolvable conundrum.

The worst of it was she knew damn well he'd already thought through all these possibilities, scenarios, options, and eventualities.

Wendy checked her watch, wiping the condensation from the face. It was too early for even the coffee stands but the timer on their machine would have a dark, earthy blend ready and filling the house with a rich aroma of morning.

She climbed the steps and let herself in. Jay was already awake, drinking her coffee and reading the paper which had likely just arrived by way of the delivery boy with an arm the Braves would probably one day find invaluable. He never missed their four-by-four porch ten plus feet in the air. Most times it was lying there dead center and the two of them had never caught him using the stairs.

He rarely slowed down on his BMX.

"Morning, baby," Wendy said.

"Hey you—sorry I dove into the coffee. I know there's something about that first cup but I didn't sleep well last night and that *ambrosial* aroma literally abducted me and forced my hand. I'm not even sure I'm myself yet and this is my second cup."

"Ambrosial. Big words don't impress me, Professor. I will, however, give you points for alliteration and the quality of the word itself. Next time just give me the two dollar word, okay?"

"You got it."

"Besides, you're going to make it up to me tonight with your world famous lasagna. And candles."

She crossed the living room and dropped onto his lap, causing the near-full cup of opaque goodness to spill on Hanson's house pants.

Wendy cleaned up the last of the lasagna, rinsed the dishes, and put them in the dishwasher. Jay was in the shower, preparing for a night lecture at the Law School, which would give her time to think about all that had happened over the previous three years and whether or not she wanted to accept the proposal of marriage her boyfriend had just given over Italian food, wine, and a croissant with an engagement ring tied to it with a crimson-colored ribbon.

Wendy met the professor, retired and infamous trial lawyer J.W. Hanson, when taking one of his non-law classes and after awkwardly asking him to defend her uncle—the man charged with killing her own mother. She'd almost immediately fallen in love with him, even after disbelieving such dramatics of "love at first sight" before. The chemistry was instantaneous and completely undeniable and she fought it at first. Hard. But it was like taking on an angry bull: losing the battle was not a matter of "if" but rather a matter of "when."

Since that time, three years earlier, Wendy and her prodigal father had reconciled. It was not because of her mother's death or at least not only so. She loved her father very much—always had. Now here Wendy was, faced with a proposal from a man she loved (and loved as deeply as she loved Pruett, her newly reborn father, albeit in a resplendently different way), and perhaps she even faced yet a different name change, depending on what she said and did.

Wendy had always believed another marriage was not for her. People could make all arguments to the contrary but she felt there was something about the sanctioning—the legality of it all, ironically—that changed something.

Saying the vows in front of a congregation, having a total stranger preside over it and the state legitimizing it with blood tests and the signatures of witnesses—for her it stole the innocence, spontaneity, romance, and even encroached on the bond of love.

What could be stronger than what one heart felt for another? What could solidify two people being together for the rest of their lives more perfectly than—

The front door to J.W. Hanson's apartment burst open and two masked figures exploded into the room from the shadows outside. One had his arms around Wendy before she could think to put up a fight and the other stuffed a gag in her mouth and pulled a hood over her head. As they whisked her away from the apartment, Wendy writhing and twisting, she could still hear the shower water running in the other room. Then there was a bee sting on her left shoulder and she went to sleep wondering if proposals left hanging in the air, unaccepted, remained promises at all.

Omar had not felt so alive in many years. It was not that the transformation inside him had abandoned him—far from it—the feeling of weakness toward his profession, the acts he performed with excellence, only morphed with the new self.

Working on the unsavory man, Skylar Durden, the betrayer of friends, had helped Omar to see that he was simply at a crossroads in life. God had meant him to see his own reflection as prodigal father mirrored back in the pleading face of Tim Mackay. He would complete his work here—whatever needed to be done, without any further hesitation—and then he would talk to Cristóbal; make him understand that *familia* was most important and that he needed to find his son and make amends. That was his future; finding the money amongst these children was *now*.

The boy, Durden, had confessed quite early on that he also betrayed Rachel's confidence one evening while smoking marijuana with two friends—a Frank Purdy and Gus Illson. Of course the two laughed at him, thinking he was playing a prank, but Durden was convincing. The three had then smoked more and more of the pot, making up dreams as to what each would do with so much money until they eventually passed out.

The next day they said their goodbyes and Durden told Omar he thought little of it, believing that if his friends remembered anything at all (which was unlikely considering the amount they had smoked) they would think his story was a fantasy.

Omar accepted that he was destined to follow this trail of stupid children to the pot of gold. Durden had no reason to lie, but Omar spent several hours with the boy, a knife, and a glowing warmth inside him doing things that by his own definitions made Omar feel more himself than he had in a time.

He buried the body. He could not afford to allow the lawman—Pruett—to follow the same trail as he. It was time to be more careful. Ultimately it was the only way back to his son.

Sheriff Pruett knocked lightly on Jesse Claremont's door. The same house in which he'd once cheated on his wife; the same house where he'd made love to Jesse in the months following his wife's death, thinking that though his previous affair with her could be blamed on all the booze, he might actually have feelings for her.

In the end, the sponsor/addict role made for the best friendship they'd ever had. And it had rescued Pruett from his demons—the kind that beckoned remorselessly from inside a bottle, anyway—more than a few times.

Jesse opened the door dressed in jeans and a t-shirt, barefoot, and with a large steaming cup of dark, rich coffee in her hands. She held the cup out to Pruett and he accepted it as if he'd waited all his life for *that* coffee.

"Come in," Jesse said. "You need to tell me everything that happened."

Pruett sat down at the kitchen table and told her about interviewing Val Beard, the whiskey bottle within his grasp, the smell of the alcohol mixed with the other man's odor and the smells of the kitchen, the way the animal inside him awoke and wanted to be sated.

"But you didn't accept his offer of a drink," she told him.

"No."

"And that's how we get by, James. Moment by moment; day by day."

"I don't know what I might have done—where I might have gone—if you hadn't picked up the phone."

"We've all had moments like that. And we'll have them again. The thing is we don't live our lives on what ifs and could haves or any of the other crap. Our actions are what matter, James. What you did, *that matters.*"

She stood up from the table, leaned over his large frame, and hugged him tight. "You need to be as proud of yourself as I am of you in this moment."

"What happened between us?" Pruett said when she'd returned to her seat, eyes wet, cheeks flush like roses.

"We had a bad beginning. Good things don't come from bad beginnings that often. We were two drunks, each looking for someone to tell us what we were doing was okay."

"You know I don't mean *then.*"

"I know you don't. But we tried to pick things up without the original problems ever being fixed," she said.

Pruett's cell rang. It was J.W. Hanson.

"Professor Hanson, are you still taking good care of my daughter?"

"I don't know where she is, James."

Pruett felt the blood drain from his face. "What are you talking about, Jay?"

"We'd just eaten; I was showering. When I came out, she wasn't here. Her car is still parked downstairs."

"How long has it been? Maybe she walked to a store—"

"It's been three hours."

"Jesus," Pruett whispered, and the animal inside growled. "Have you called the Laramie police?"

"I know they'll wait at least a full day. In fact, they'll ask enough questions to find out I had just proposed to her and they'll hold back their smirks and think she hightailed it for the hills. I called you because you know your daughter. She doesn't run from anything."

"I'll call the Chief of Police there. We've talked at a couple of conferences. I can get him to put out BOLOs now. You stay right there in case she comes back."

Pruett disconnected.

"Oh my God, James."

"It's worse than that," Pruett said. "This isn't random."

His cell rang again, this time with a blocked number.

"Pruett."

"Mijo," the familiar, nameless voice said.

"I won't stop until there's nothing left of you," Pruett said. "You cartel pieces of shit aren't the only ones who know how to take a body apart."

"If you don't want to start receiving parts of your precious little girl in the mail, I'd stop now."

Pruett said nothing.

"I gave you a week. You still have five days left. I only want you to think of this as an insurance policy. Your daughter has seen nothing, knows no one, and we'll keep it that way."

"You'll let her go?"

"If you bring us the money, we'll let her go. If you don't, we'll test your theory on who knows what about body parts."

The phone disconnected.

"I have to go," Pruett said.

"I think it's more important than ever that you take a few breaths, drink some more coffee, and decompress," Jesse said.

Pruett could see in her eyes she knew how impotent the words were in such a situation, but he barked at her anyway. "My Wendy is in the hands of the Sustantivo drug cartel," Pruett said. "The last thing on earth I would do is jeopardize her safe return by crawling into any bottle."

Jesse nodded and stood with him. She wrapped her arms around him and kissed him deeply. "I've always loved you, Sheriff."

"I'm sorry to snap at you. You are my rock, Jess. I'm going to make all of this right again."

"I'll be here. I've always been here, James."

Rob Underwood had been working as a United States Forestry Service ranger for three and a half months. As a rookie, he pulled five days a week at the Green River Lakes station where his job all day long was babysitting mosquito-bitten hikers who were either lost, angry, psychotic, or all of the above. He was also responsible for making sure all outfitters (or anyone else with a horse, for that matter) had a valid permit to take the animal(s) into the wilderness and for doing an inspection upon their exodus from the Highline Trail.

It was not unusual to see outfitters off and not witness them come out. The Highline Trail was just over thirty miles long and came out at another major trailhead, where there was another ranger station. If an outfitter's planned trip was one-way they were to declare it, then Rob's job was to radio or call the ranger stationed at the other end and let them know the license and other information of the riders who would be coming out on the southern end and when.

So when the tall Latino man walked into the smoldering little A-frame hut Rob Underwood thought it was starting off like any other day—with a confused hiker that would likely speak to him in broken English about one problem or another, either of which the junior ranger would have no ability to solve even when he did finally understand the nature of the issue.

"This is the trailhead for the Highline Trail, yes?" Omar said.

"Yes. The trail is just over thirty miles long and parallels the majestic Wind River—"

"I noticed you allow horse trailers, so that means people are allowed to take horses on the trail?"

"Yes, with the proper permits."

"And you must sign these horses in—or, rather, the people *with* the horses?"

"Every one of them," said Underwood, wondering now if this were some type of inspection or check-up on his knowledge of the rules. The man was clearly of Latin descent but he spoke excellent English. "We sign them in and out, whichever end of the trail they utilize for entry and exit."

"May I see your records for the last three weeks?"

"You can if you drive back to town and stop in the Sheriff's Office. We just printed that list for them earlier today. One from each ranger station. Or you can have them issue you a secondary request. The information is not for the public—unless you have some credentials."

"Credentials?"

"From the Forest Service, maybe?"

"No. I would just like the information. I was thinking maybe we could help each other."

"How's that?"

"You give me the print out and I don't kill you."

Rob stood there, dumbfounded for a moment. Then he realized he was being hazed. Some kind of rookie joke.

"That's funny," Rob said.

"I don't think it's funny at all," said Omar and drew his 9 MM pistol, pointing it at the ranger's head.

"Sh-shit, man, joke's over. Not funny is right. Fuck this shit."

"Do you have family, Mr. Ranger?"

"Yes."

"Married, perhaps?"

"Yes."

"What is your last name?"

"Underwood."

Omar motioned toward the computer screen with the end of the handgun. "Do not make Mrs. Underwood a widow today. Print out a list just as you did for Sheriff Pruett. You are connected electronically to the ranger station on the other end?"

"Y-yes."

"Print that list, too."

Ranger Underwood selected the criteria on his computer and sent the output to the laser printer on his desk. He stapled the sheets of paper together.

Omar took the papers and leaned in close, making eye contact with the young man behind the counter, showing him the soul behind his own eyes; the soul capable of sending him backwards with a bullet in his head. "Your wife is a lucky woman," Omar said.

Then he left without another word.

Zach Canter called Sheriff Pruett and asked him to come back to the station where they could talk in his office.

"What's up, Zachary?"

"I followed up on those outfitters—seemed like legitimate clients, just hired to visit the mountains up close."

"Good work."

"I've been thinking, Sheriff," Zach said.

"Uh-oh."

"Shriver and Purdy, the horse riders who got their mounts from the Beards. A ranch hand and a rock climber? They're town guys, and they *are* good friends—part of a dope-smoking lot. Drinkers, too. Shriver works mostly in the gas fields. Not my favorite guy in town but pretty harmless. Same with Purdy. I just figured a guy with access to mountain horses goes up with a rock climber during our three-week window—seems more than coincidence."

"I told you before you're a good cop, Deputy. This is the first solid lead we've gotten. Outstanding police work, son."

"Thanks, boss."

Pruett drove straight to Keil Shriver's one-room house in the Sandstone subdivision. He pounded on the door but the house was dark and no one answered. He tried two other homes—that of Reb Norman and another, where the climbers Illson and Purdy rented. At the rental a neighbor who had just pulled in the driveway next door waved the sheriff down as he was returning to his vehicle.

"I haven't seen those two clowns in *a week*. At least. Normally there's ganja smoke pouring out the chimney and I'm over there every other night asking them to turn the music down. Over a week, ten days? Nothing."

"Thanks," Pruett said. He called into dispatch and Melody Munney answered. "Mel, get everyone out in their cars and an APB for all four of those young men: Keil Shriver, Reb Norman, Frank Purdy, and Gussy Illson. I don't care where you all find them; get 'em to the station and don't let them go until I've had a chance to talk to them. If they ask you tell them it's for their own good—protective custody. Lock them up and watch your own back, too, understood?"

"Yes, sir," Deputy Munney said.

Pruett got on his cell and called Malcolm. "I need your help. Can you come into town and meet me at the town park?"

"Town park?"

"I need to know we're alone, Mal. No outside ears at all."

"Be there in half an hour."

Pruett drove to the town park and found it deserted. The night brought with it the chill of the north when the sun went down, even in summer.

He knew where the money was. Knew it in his gut—the gut instinct. A cop's best friend. And he knew there was only one way to get the money without inside or outside law enforcement. Only one. He sat in his Suburban and debated making a call he knew he had no choice but to make. He hoped somehow that questioning it would bring him to a place of moral equity with the rest of the world but he knew that was not possible, even without the call.

War changes those who fight it. While every person reacts differently and comes home in a variety of different physical and mental states, there is something that all soldiers who have witnessed the real thing and survived have.

Whether it's the growth of a metaphysical organ or a psychological awakening, these veterans of homicide realize that the world that is seen by most is but a veneer, kindly placed by the maker or by accident, but by whom or why doesn't end up mattering.

Not unlike the Wizard of Oz—once a person has been behind the curtain, they know the greatest kept secret (and horror) of all:

Humans are capable of ANYTHING.

Most want to live in a world where ghosts are not real and horrible realities such as AIDS and famine and torture and slow death affect other people in other countries and the average citizen only wants to know why their morning paper is late or what the latest flavor of latté tastes like.

And Pruett knew it *should* be that way. One human being suffering is a tragedy but it doesn't mean that another human being should suffer, too. A starving child in a war-torn nation dreams of food, not of another human losing their food so that he or she may eat.

But what most *don't* understand is that things must be done in the name of freedom, in the name of protection, in the name of love, and in the name of the greater good that otherwise might seem immoral taken out of humanitarian context.

Pruett made the call.

Keil Shriver's eyes were closed, though he had been coherent enough to hear the sheriff knocking on the door before, earlier. He was also bound, naked, covered in red gashes and crimson splotching where he'd been punched many times, and gagged so he could not answer.

"We're not quite finished here," Omar told him. "I feel like talking and resting. You are a strong man—like your cousins, no? Not so strong inside, though—it is from there I have always measured a man or woman.

"I pondered whether to come here to speak with you at all, can you imagine that? Nearly my second terrible mistake. You see, Keil, I am a purveyor of men—I study them, find their weaknesses, their fears—and then I become an exploiter of those treasures which I find. I am not an investigator by trade. But when I saw your name on the list along with the Purdy man—you taking horses into the mountains—I was certain I had put together the plan."

Omar noticed the surprise on his captive's face.

"Oh yes, your friend Durden, he told me everything before he died. Well, except the—what you call it? Crisscross? No, no—*double-cross*—you people, so unlike mine. None of you can be trusted. Tim's Rachel betrays him, both physically and with the money; Durden turns to Illson and Purdy, who of course need their good friend Keil to get horses and take them in and out of the wilderness to capture their own fortune. But you? The final betrayer. Maybe this is fitting as you may very likely be the last in this sordid web of lying and stealing and murdering that I myself will have to kill—"

Shriver began begging—or trying to through his gag—but the sounds only made Omar smile. "I believe I will let Rachel live. Of you all, I still feel she should suffer the most. Does that make any sense to you? I told you before, during our talks, how taken I was by her boyfriend—by Tim.

"Do you know what I will be doing with the rest of my life, Keil? It may help you as you go on to whatever comes next after *this* life to hear that I am going to find my son—my boy whom I've not contacted in years—and I am going to embrace him, and cry, and I am going to pray that he loves me and forgives me and I am going to ask him if he would like to learn how to build ships.

"Years before the army and the cartel I did know a craft. I would like to retire in southern Mexico, South America, or even the Caribbean, and build ships with my son. Boats we could sell to the fishermen and rent out to tourists. Boats in which we could go out when we like and fish ourselves."

Omar looked at Keil, motionless, without the ability any longer to make noises. Perhaps dead already. Omar stopped cleaning and sharpening the bayonet knife. "This, Keil—this hopeful future—it makes me happy. So does this."

And he drove the blade into the young man's kidney.

Whitefeather and the sheriff sat on a bench in the descending cold of night.

"You called Rhys?" Whitefeather finally said.

"I had to. It's my daughter, Mal. A fucking Mexican drug cartel has my little girl. What the hell else would warrant a call to Rhys if not that?"

"You have a point. Rhys is still doing what he does?"

"Yes."

"And he has people that can assist."

"They'll deploy tonight and be here in the morning."

"How many?"

"Including Rhys? Twenty-five."

"Jesus."

"It's not even a platoon," Pruett said.

"These guys redefine the numbers, Jimmy, ten to one. You know that truth as well as I do. Look, I get the gravity of the situation," Whitefeather said. "But I'm still not sure how bringing in Rhys and his mercenaries gives you more leverage."

"First, we have to get to the money," Pruett said. "You know the Beards. They're shit rotten to the core and they have at least fifteen hands working for them that wouldn't be there if they weren't armed and dangerous. Most of 'em are pot growers and killers, not ranch hands."

"So you think the bags of money are at the Beard place?"

"I can't tell you yet how it all played itself out, but these climbers—Purdy and Illson—maybe they found the money. Maybe Tim and Rachel found it and got them involved. Whatever happened, whoever told whom, Purdy talked Shriver into taking the horses into the Winds to pack the money out. We know that much from the records Zach brought down. I think everyone involved underestimated the Beards and how they would've figured something was going on and I think they *definitely* underestimated what the Beard brothers would be capable of when a ton of money was at stake. Hell, the *Beards* might not have known what they were capable of. Greed makes a damn tempting lover."

"But is that all you have—supposition, good instincts, but what else?"

"A neighbor of Purdy and Illson hasn't seen them there in ten days."

"So?"

"Said he's over there every single night telling them to turn down the music and put away the bong. I checked where they work, over at the feed store, loading bags. They're fired. Never called in, just quit showing up."

"You think they're dead," said Whitefeather.

"I think they're buried out on that ranch with the money. Shriver and Norman I'm not sure about. Keil, he's a cousin, but I didn't get the sense Val has much use for him."

"Okay, so these men that are coming—"

"Two are females," Pruett said.

"Okay, these *soldiers* that are coming to help, you figure you storm the Beard place and get them to give up the money?"

"I can't send in my own deputies. Can't have that on my conscience. Let's be real here: this is ransom money we're talking about now. And the source is a drug cartel."

"It still seems like overkill," Whitefeather said.

"You haven't heard the second part of my plan. These men who hold my daughter captive, they don't respect anything but their own ways; their own methodology."

"So what does that mean?"

"So that means once we have the money, we set up the exchange and we teach them a lesson."

"And you think this *helps* your chances of getting Wendy back alive?"

"These people give bodies back. That's it. Dumb country fucksticks like me, we're supposed to fall right into line and believe these coldblooded murderers when they tell us to do as they say and we'll see our loved ones again. You and I, Mal, we've *been to war.* You don't think they'll give her back to me, do you?"

"No."

"Then what's so confusing about all this to you? I figured you of all people would understand—"

"I *do* understand. 'Course I understand. I just don't know if starting a war with a drug cartel benefits anyone— including you, Wendy, and the rest of Wind River."

"If we send the right message it might."

"If we send the wrong message they might have to do a new state map and remove our town and this whole damn valley from it."

"I've thought this through. But I need you *and* your expertise. I also need your counsel, friendship, and belief in me, or I won't be able to go through with this, and certainly not *sober*."

"Oh, Christ on a lily pad…always the drama from you. Jimmy Pruett, if you asked me right now to go out to the train tracks, lie down, and let the next locomotive run me over, I'd do it for you. Doesn't mean I wouldn't ask why, or want to talk it through. Tell me the rest of your plan, white man. Then we'll put a little Injun twist to it and maybe, just maybe, it'll look like somethin' then."

Pruett clasped his old friend on the shoulder and then began unloading his mind.

Pruett and Whitefeather knew Rhys from British Special Forces. Rhys was a Commander but also the best sniper in the Brits' Corp. The line about war changing a person, that's a cliché, but it's also the simplest way to say it. A more complicated way is to say that the horror and the lack of humanity that one sees everywhere from a street corner to the market to the jungle to the sands eternal—all of it rooted in the same feral, uncivilized, brutal ancestors that live inside us all—burrows its way into the soul and it spreads from there like a cancer.

And just like a cancer, some are able to survive it. Doesn't mean it's not still there—they call it remission, much as the drunk calls sobriety a state, not a victory. Some succumb to the cancer and, in the case of a veteran, cannot live any longer with waking up sweaty and screaming, or living with a loaded firearm beneath their pillow (if they slept in their house or their bed at all, many instead curling up on the cold floor with their rifles, as they did in the bush or the sand or the mud), or seeing the blank scream in their mind and facing the most terrible moment, when the projector begins rolling and the images start playing across the whiteness.

Those who cannot survive the cancer, they end it. Some eat a bullet; others drive off a cliff. Some have been strung out on drugs so long they simply up the dosage; take a hotshot.

Other men and women who were particularly good at what they did overseas turn a different way. They become who they were trained to become. In a strange way, Pruett always believed, they were the normal ones. Every soldier—Marine, Army, any infantry person sent to the shit—before they were airmailed into Hell—were trained to be merciless killers when the time for it came. You could not send a young boy or girl into the maw of senselessness and murder and torture and fire without turning their brain into a computer that knew how to serve up whoop-ass when required.

Soldiers like Rhys Solleveld and his team of mercs; they simply carried on the fucking tradition—as Rhys would put it. And Pruett understood Rhys still; understood his heart. Some mercenaries were for hire to the largest bidder. Rhys and his crew, yes, they did what they did for a living, but they only accepted work to fight on the side of causes they considered justified. It was a fine line sometimes, Pruett knew—much of the time – but they fought for freedom and the end of repression and rape and murder and tyranny, not just the largest bank check.

And Pruett had no truck with that at all.

Pruett, Whitefeather, Rhys Solleveld, and the rest of Rhys's crew—code-named Insertion Team Osprey—were gathered in the sheriff's kitchen, only a mile or so as the crow flew, from the team's objective, the Beard ranch.

"I've taken into account what you've told me, James, regarding your feeling the money is on the Beard ranch along with perhaps some number of dead bodies. I'd like to suggest a reconnaissance tonight to attempt a location of both."

"I have no issues with that," said Pruett. "Could make the rest simpler."

"Exactly," said Solleveld. "We'll not be concerned with the bodies," he told his team, "but my hope is that the money will be nearby. Team Osprey will be dressed in full gear, night-painted, and masked. You're all fluent in several languages, but I hand-selected you because your Spanish dialects are impeccable.

"On recon, all communication, no matter how low or presumed undetectable, I want to be in Spanish— preferably of northern territory dialect. We don't intend on being heard but if we are, remember Team Osprey is a bunch sent by the Mexican cartel. If we locate the money, we leave it untouched. The next night we'll scoop it up. Dexter and Garcia," he said specifically to a pair on the team, "if we find the money on recon, you'll remain behind on surveillance for twenty-four hours to make sure the objective remains in place."

"If you *don't* find the cash tonight?" Pruett said.

"Then the mission becomes one of kill and capture. We'll have to keep the Beard brothers alive long enough to extract the location of the objective. If we find the money tonight, tomorrow night is strike and destroy, retrieving the objective of course."

"And if the Beards get frisky and move the cash?"

"We'll intercept, take out the transport, return them to the ranch, and continue tomorrow night with strike and destroy," Solleveld said.

If the money wasn't found on the reconnaissance mission, Pruett knew what Rhys meant by "extract" the location of the money. Tim Mackay would've known it all too well, were he still alive to tell it. The team would go to work on the Beard brothers, extricating the information as to where the drug money was. When they had their answers, like the cartel, they would finish them off. Pruett didn't care for that part of the plan—nor any of the violence against the Beards and their crew—but he knew it was essential. To get the money without the scent of local involvement, the evidence in the aftermath needed to point to the cartel.

When they had retrieved the money and destroyed the ranch, Rhys would radio Pruett who would let the fire do its job. Around dawn, Pruett would call his deputies and tell them something had gone down at the Beard ranch and they needed to meet at the turnout on Highway 191 to Flat Top Mountain, gather, plan, and then move in on the ranch. Pruett would guide his team as delicately as possible. He'd promised himself to stay as long as he could; this would be a profound moment—just as long ago Pruett had been party to the discovery of the illegal aliens—men, women, and children—left to rot in the Wyoming flatlands by greedy men like those who operated the drug cartels. These things burned a brand into the soul that could never be removed and Pruett swore he'd be there for his deputies.

Only this time Pruett would counsel his deputies hypocritically—he would live, knowing their personal moments of professional shock—the ones burned indelibly on their souls—and the horror that would torment them, waking them in the night, hitting them from out of nowhere without warning, was of his own design.

Chapter 7

THE SHERIFF station was empty. Pruett had five days remaining before he had to return blood money to the cartel or risk the arrival of the first package with a piece of his baby girl in it. Oaths, morals, logic, past, future—they all made terrible paths to the hidden answer of what to do. There are many times in a life when a person must choose *what to do*. But rarely—never, if one is fortunate—does that same decision take on a life-altering, overpowering importance. It becomes not a question one can ask of another but only inward, to the soul, because it is the soul that will live with the answer for the rest of a man's life.

When James Pruett ran for the office of Sheriff over two decades earlier, he did not do so out of political motivation or as wood to the fire of a raging ego. He did so because of his love for Wind River: its quiet majesty; its unmatched camaraderie; its dying traditions. Across the country even smaller towns were in moral decay. Crime was spreading everywhere. Pruett truly believed in the oath he swore because the words in the oath best described his reasons for wanting to be a sheriff.

To protect, serve, and keep safe his constituency while upholding the standards of honesty, decency, and lawfulness of the community.

Was handing back very likely tens of millions in cartel money serving the community or only his own crumbling heart? That money would eventually further fuel the drug infestation that was likely going to catalyze the ultimate ending to the grand human experiment.

But the sheriff did not doubt that the very, very bad men meant what they said when they told him they would burn his town to ashes. As the man with no name had made clear, the threat wasn't metaphor. He'd read up on the cartels of Mexico in the twenty-first century. They ruled by overwhelming any resistance (or perceived resistance). The tactic had always been a brilliant one. Shock and awe; leave your opponent so stunned, jaws agape, that never again would the possibility of betrayal ever enter their weakened mind again.

Sustantivo, in particular, ruled their countryside through sheer terror. It was not eye-for-an-eye with them; it was body-for-an-eye, town-for-a-body with them. And their view of what constituted "their countryside" seemed to grow daily.

And that was really the crux of the decision at which he ultimately arrived. Wind River was not going to fall to the Sustantivo cartel. And just as the bad men had no intention of returning Wendy to him alive, Pruett knew they intended to teach this small town in the middle of Wyoming—this tiny place thousands of miles from the eye of their evil storm—a lesson. One they would expect to resonate with other small, remote and seemingly unrelated, untouchable places in the world.

We can come for you, too.

And so Sheriff James Pruett had made the terribly troubling decision to fight the cartel on their terms. In Vietnam the U.S. won very few ground battles using strictly U.S. techniques, modes, and training. The engagements that they won—significant victories against the enemy—were those in which their own platoons were willing to resort to the tactics and methodology of the jungle enemy.

Play them on *their* field.

It was the only chance Pruett figured they had. He only hoped his sacrifice could be chosen—that he could die instead of any around him who followed him into the nightmare of his plans. Wendy. If he could save his town *and* her, then to hell with the rest. Morality and other peoples' wishes and problems and opinions would have to take the back seat. Sheriff Pruett's job was to soldier for his own town and people.

But Wind River was the kind of place where people looked out for their friends, neighbors, and community. Pruett was counting on it. What he didn't know was how much to tell and to whom. If a fire breaks out in a crowded room, yeah, you need to get peoples' butts outta there, but if you scream FIRE, you're likely to start a stampede, killing children, the elderly, and anyone else who falls to the ground.

It seemed as if life was a perpetual balancing act and Pruett was the one without a net. It was times like that the crushing need to drink overwhelmed him. It did not come from one place within his body but rather from all places at once. Every pore exuded the smell of the finest whiskey he'd ever drank; every muscle reminded him how loose and warm and ready for battle the alcohol made him.

Of course it had nothing to do with his heart or soul or muscles or any other part of his body talking to him. Mind games. Addiction. It could take on many looks, many feels, many faces, but it was the same wretched beast that waited patiently for years at a time, looking for that one crack, that single tiny fissure through which his addiction could begin to suck the will and pride and courage from within.

He knew he needed to reveal his plan in a place where a black sheriff was not always welcomed with open arms and kindly hearts. But it was the location that served his need, and he couldn't do anything without the backbone of courage of the people of Stone Creek, Wyoming. There were hundreds of them, each one tougher than the last, it sometimes seemed.

It was one of those towns that was difficult to think of as a town at all. Stone Creek was a conglomeration of ranches with a gas station/store/bar right on the main highway. It was easily the largest collection of conservative ranchers in the world, spread over thousands of acres and most related to the other in one way or another. The surnames there were few and prolific. The McIntyre ranch where Sheriff Pruett's Bethy died from a gunshot wound to the head was in Stone Creek.

Pruett did not receive many votes in the elections from the area of Stone Creek, in part because many of the ranchers did not vote, some being old enough that the outcomes did not matter much to them, others because whichever way the town of Wind River voted was the way things would be (Wind River by comparison was an urban metropolis). There were not a lot of people in the Wind River area who had ever flinched at the idea of a black sheriff in an almost entirely white part of the state, but most who did lived in the Stone Creek area.

The other thing that existed in Stone Creek was what Pruett had grown up calling the Stone Creek Slough, others simply the Stone Creek Bridge. It was directly on Highway 191, the only primary road in or out of Wind River once having passed the "Sage cut-off" road to the south, a roundabout way to swing back through Sage, Wyoming and into Wind River from the north/northwest, still on Highway 191.

The Stone Creek Valley was the first area driving northward where one knew he or she was entering the unfettered grandeur of the Rocky Mountains. Until then, seventy or more miles of crackling asphalt north of Interstate 80 was about as flat as a road could be. Just after passing the Sage cut-off, you dropped into a valley full of trees and watered tributaries and thick willow bushes that in the fall would have you shaking your head and wondering how there could not be a God and that He was not an artist.

A few miles after entering the valley, the highway dropped rather severely, just after the store and bar, into the slough's deep pocket. Once a vehicle had crossed the bridge itself northbound or southbound, it climbed back out of the slough rather quickly. An even more unusual element of the slough was that there was a second bridge that mirrored the first in everything but age and technology. It sat due west of the more sturdy and traveled bridge, about fifty yards. There were swing-down dirt roads that veered off the highway and then back on again.

Sheriff Pruett planned on making the old Stone Creek Bridge and the slough itself into the Little Bighorn, with the hired killers that had been sent north playing the part of Custer's Cavalry and the ranchers of Stone Creek and Sage and other outlying areas and whatever citizens of Wind River that chose to play the part of Crazy Horse and his band of Sioux. But first, Pruett had to make his case in front of the people of Stone Creek. He needed to instill in them the gravity of what was happening and how it threatened their land.

To all people in Wyoming, land was important. To the rancher, land was beyond sacred. The land was like a second bride every rancher married when he or she decided to stake down a life there. Most inherited that life, and many had no choices in the matter, but that didn't make the relevance of the land any less real or palpable.

And for the most part, like the majority of small communities (Wind River included, though not to the same extent), Stone Creek residents mistrusted strangers at best. And these were mostly innocent and friendly people with no ill will toward Stone Creek or its township or the land whatsoever. The residents were simply introverted and careful by nature.

Pruett called the meeting in the smallish Community Center, a decrepit, white, wood-sided building that served as church, square-dance hall, meeting place, and even a safe party place for underage teens to drink and pass out with a sleeping bag, some alone, some with a warm body next to them—the main idea being no young ones driving home drunk.

"Quiet, you all, please. Quiet down."

The ranchers jawing with each other and mostly ignoring Sheriff Pruett until then stopped talking and turned squarely to face their presenter. Respect and proper manner and a tradition of rote were ingrained with the people of the land as much as the traditions of the first race that settled the area.

"Most of you do not know why I have called you here. I'm going to keep it simple. We're all of us a unpretentious people who like the facts and not a lot of fluff, so it seems best we keep it that way."

A few agreeable chuckles and "damn rights."

Pruett continued.

"There is a blight that has set itself on our community. One that never should have showed its ugly face this far north and never, ever in our proud community here in Stone Creek, Wind River, and the surrounding vicinities. This is where our children grow and go to school and date and drive the roads. This blight—these people, if they can be referred to as such; these *animals*, have descended on our town out of greed.

"Now greed's not a sin unknown to any of us here. We're human. But no one with whom I'm familiar in this room—and that's every goddamned one of you, by the way—is either capable of or would ever consider doing, much less traveling a thousand miles to *do* what has been done in Wind River.

"A young man by the name of Tim Mackay—some of you know him; some of you do not—was tortured and murdered in his own home in Wind River two nights ago."

There was an instant murmur in the room, a few chairs sliding wood against wood, some because a person had known Tim, others because of what such a terrible action implied to everyone in the room and, indeed, community. Some were moved because it was both.

"This is a time to set down differences," Pruett continued. "These men—I've met one of them—they are very bad men. They truly are animals. They torture and kill young people with no more thought or remorse than you or I would step on a bug. Less, in fact."

"Who are these men, Sheriff?" said Maisy Jensen, one of the eldest Jensens who populated over a third of Stone Creek Valley and ranged in age from several months to a hundred years. Maisy was eighty-nine and Sheriff Pruett would not care to arm-wrestle her even on a good day. "Who are these creatures who ain't got the respect for life or land?"

"Ma'am—"

"Goddamn it, James, you call me Maisy or by all that's righteous I will come up there and pin your ears back. Your mother and I drank coffee and a spit of whiskey every Saturday afternoon until the day she passed and I will not be put to shame by her son calling me *ma'am*, respectfully as it may be intended. Besides, you say ma'am and I turn and look for my mama, who only died just last year at one hundred and nine and a half years young."

"My apologies, Maisy. I remember you and my mother drinking, well, let's call it Wyoming coffee and be done with it."

Maisy smiled and nodded her approval. It was a dance you did with such people. They had *lived* and you never forgot that; you never ignored what they had to say because every sentence contained either a pearl of wisdom, a funny story, or most times both.

"The men we speak of are drug dealers. And they come from a cartel south in Arizona and Mexico called Sustantivo. It means, translated roughly and as they intend it, 'the best' or 'the greatest'. Either way, I've come to ask for your help."

Robby McClintock stood and said, "Murder. Is that what you're suggestin', Sheriff Pruett? Murder plain and simple?"

McClintock was no fan of Sheriff James Pruett and he didn't care who knew it either. But there was no arguing the point. He *was* asking the community for just that— pure, coldblooded killing. For a hopefully equivalent cause, but that didn't change a thing about the means.

"Ain't going to stand up here and tell you a piece of bull dung is a biscuit, Robby, if that's what you're getting at. I never said it was pretty and I won't say it isn't murder. But I'm thinking there isn't any of you that wouldn't kill one of these bastards if they were on your doorstep threatening your families and what I'm suggesting—and hear this loud and clear, every one of ya—is that they *will* be there, on your doorstep, but then it'll be too late."

Burr Swift stood up and pointed a bony finger at the sheriff, but he stared at Robby McClintock as he spoke.

"Don't care how a one of ya feel about the man standin' up there. He's kin. He's fuckin' *WYOMIN'* kin, and that's the most important kind. And if I hear a one of ya grumble or spit or even so much as shuffle at the idea of helpin' him, I'll beat the shit out of ya right here and right fuckin' now."

There were some "yeahs" and some grumbling but for the most part it seemed the room got the point.

Billy Snow stood—twenty-year-old son of Bert Snow and a rancher for his father. "But is it, Sheriff? Is what you've come here to ask us for is to murder these cartel men, in cold blood?"

"It is, son," Pruett said. "And if you could know my heart, I'd never ask it in a million years—'specially of a young man such as yourself—if I didn't believe at my core it was the only way to save our land, our towns, and our way of life."

Billy Snow nodded. "Then I'm in, sir. With everything I got."

Complete silence descended on the room. No one spoke up an objection. Burr Swift was ninety if he was a day, and frankly Pruett thought of him as more than a little racist, but he'd defended the sheriff and after Billy spoke you couldn't have torn the wood-toothed smile from him with a chainsaw.

It infused Pruett with an inferno of pride to hear such words and to witness such congregation. But there was more.

"There's something I haven't told you," Pruett said. "I don't want to make this personal because I don't want you to feel you're being asked to participate in a personal favor or action. You all know my daughter Wendy. She's in Laramie now, if you didn't know it, and last night cartel thugs broke into where she hangs her hat and took her away."

The room gasped collectively.

"They have told me if I do not return to them the money that went down in the crashed airplane in the mountains by Friday, they will begin sending her to me by parcel, and in pieces."

There was more silence after that. Pruett had to turn from the crowd and wipe at his eyes. Saying the words had been too much to bear, as he'd feared. When he turned, Maisy Jensen was next to him on the stage, extending her arms wide. Pruett, the hulk of a man, the prideful sheriff, fell into them and wept.

When he faced the crowd again his eyes were red but dry again.

"I swear to you on my Bethy's love that if it were any other member of this community I would be asking the same thing, no difference. I ain't saying this doesn't strike me deeper. Not implying that at all. Of course it does. What I'm swearing to you is that as much as possible I've not allowed it to cloud my judgment and that as Sheriff of Sublette County. You all are my sons and daughters, too, as is the land, our town, and everything we each love here in our home. Just that Wendy's included in that, and I see no other way to chase away the evil that has landed here so that it doesn't come back. Not ever."

Jonesy Shriver, who got his name from the granddaddy on his mother's side and who was cousin to the as yet unannounced murdered young man in Wind River, chaired the council in Stone Creek. He stood and shuffled sideways through the seated residents, then walked up to the stage. When he got there Pruett extended a hand and Shriver ignored it, moving in for a bear hug instead.

He turned to the gathering and spoke in a booming voice:

"You all git it. You know what's at stake. None of us asked fer it; none of us ask fer any of the misery that gits put down upon us. But us and every generation before us dealt with it all. The Wild West. My granddad told me the stories, passed down by his people. I call for a vote."

Bum Draper yelled, "I second."

"All in favor of takin' down this murderous scum, say 'aye'," said Jonesy Shriver.

The Stone Creek Community Center erupted in unison.

"AYE."

"Any opposed?"

Silence.

"We're in, Sheriff," he said to Pruett, and patted the lawman on the back as he relinquished the podium.

Chapter 8

THE SHERIFF eventually told the congregation of his plan. The plan for the saving of the community, his daughter, and the land by sending a message south that would not—*could not*—be misinterpreted. A message sent from the locals. The plan Malcolm Whitefeather himself had called the second coming of the Little Bighorn.

Every last local agreed. Some cheered. Others nodded solemnly, their leathered, weary faces screwed up with enough disdain to slay a hundred cartel soldiers with but a glance. Most said they would call other relatives from around the state. Each one of them trustworthy, armed, and a helluva shot.

Pruett had always been proud of his town but were he being honest with himself, it was Wind River he thought of in those moments, not the surrounding ranch communities where habits and hatred died hard. Stone Creek taught him something about the kind of people who dwelled at the *core* of the county residents he served. Not unlike Vietnam: brother lifted brother, no matter the politics in his mind, the ending of his name, or the color of his skin.

Families disagreed. Many times they broke; even shattered. But community was like family—no matter how fractured a *relationship* had been or become, when it came time to stand up and face death, you had the other's back.

Always.

Pruett sat at the kitchen table, not on the porch he built for himself and his wife. He felt unworthy of the specialness of his normal thinking place. Even though he'd broken down there before, drank from a glass of his own personal poison, desecrated the special spot out front before, this was worse. What he planned to do—no, he had to be honest; what he'd convinced his community, his *people* to do—was worse. It begged for a reckoning of the soul.

He wasn't the same man he'd been before the war; no man or woman was. But just as soldiers were a brotherhood of sorts, sharing that commonality that no other person could completely comprehend, each of them, too, were alone. They kept space with their own demons. Every man and woman who had met Death—not *seen* it, but met the loathsome creature and looked it in the eye in its most egregious of forms—was condemned to live with that introduction in their own way.

Pruett had wondered more than once in what ways his own meeting had changed him. The answer he invariably concluded was that there were too many ways to count and that he'd be forced (as all) to live a life of grisly discovery of what he was now capable; of what things he could do—for him, anyway—in the name of righteousness.

He did not kid himself. It was his own definition of righteousness, not anyone else's, and he could only hope that what he did overlapped enough with what God saw as justifiable.

And there again he was, thinking of God—a God he'd more or less dismissed completely following the war but one in whom he'd always struggled to maintain faith. Since

Bethy died, he'd found himself more forgiving of his dead father, a preacher, and his cruel ways at times of instilling "faith." Pruett wasn't Catholic, but he'd heard the cliché stories of Catholic schools and nuns with rulers and pencils.

His own father's religious weapon of choice was a razor strap, his location for delivering sermons to the flesh inside their barn, where Jimmy Pruett's mother would be less subjected (and subjugated) to the howls of her son.

Children raised in such a way—or any children, really—were not capable of separating concepts of religion and God. So many, when they reached the age of emancipation, rejected the latter for hatred of the former, and it could take many years—decades, and sometimes never—to reconcile the separation of the two.

The loss of his wife had subtly altered some cog in the machinery within Pruett's soul and he didn't quite know if it was real or only his fervent hope that the existence of God and some type of afterlife meant there was a chance for him to see his beloved wife who he missed every second of every day, no matter where he was, no matter what he was doing, asleep or awake.

Of course he understood his belief—real or manufactured—did not affect the reality of the situation. But more than just the alteration in machinery, the day he cursed God as he put Bethy in the cold Wyoming earth, he felt a profound change—profound yet only the size of a grain of sand—

Mustard seed, he heard his old man bellow from the barn.

Whatever you called it, whatever size it had been then, there was no contention that it had grown significantly since.

But then there was the bottle of Heaven Hill bourbon that sat in the center of his table, the seal holding forth the demons unbroken, as if tacky paper could hold back such creatures of the soul's destruction.

But it did. These particular demons smiled back at Pruett from inside the coppery-colored swirl of delicious drink, through the clear glass, knowing that it was *his* breaking of the seal that mattered. They waited for Pruett himself to make the choice between God and drink and when he chose the alcohol he would willingly pour the evil down into his soul, trying to fill each empty place with a soothing balm that would not last, but for a few glorious moments would make Pruett King of the whole Universe and all that resided within it. Including his Bethy—it would make him believe stronger than any faith that he could see her again.

He stared at the bottle. Two ancient warriors measuring each other for the duel ready to commence. A battle for his own soul.

Outside, Pruett heard an engine roar as it topped the apex of uneven ground leading to his cabin. Headlights swung through the darkness, then the engine died and the headlights extinguished. The sheriff instinctively placed his hand on the loaded revolver lying beside him on the table but recognized the uneven gait of the footfalls on his porch steps.

Malcolm Whitefeather did not knock. He never did. Knocking was the white man's way of admitting he had no idea about his own people, what they were up to behind a closed door (or the elk hide of a teepee flap) and whether or not they should enter or go back the way they came.

"You gonna open that bottle and get down to business?" Whitefeather said, not sitting yet, just standing there, waiting for a response.

"What business?"

"That of deconstructing yourself once again so you can get back to that other business of putting the pieces back together again."

"You want to sit down?"

"Let's sit on the porch. My ancestors fill the heavens tonight as you've never seen."

"Not feeling like I should bring my own wretchedness to such a place right now."

"Wretchedness? God almighty, man, how crazy can one white man get? Put your trust in me, Jimmy. Bring the bottle."

Whitefeather then exited to the porch.

When Pruett came out the revolver was in his belt, the bottle of Heaven Hill in his grip, still unopened. His friend leaned against the railing, staring into the sea of stars.

"When you used to tell me of this place, us hunkered in some God-forsaken patch of grass or hole dug in the mud, I thought you were just another sentimental white man who had no idea what Heaven might look like. The first time you brought me here, after the war, I knew when I retired, it would be in this town."

Pruett sat heavily in his chair and placed the gun and bottle on the table.

"Sit with me," the sheriff said.

Whitefeather turned around, shaking his head. "Can't."

"What do you mean can't?"

"No place for me at that table; not with the ghost who occupies that other chair."

"Fuck you, Malcolm."

"I'm serious, Jimmy. You called yourself 'wretched' in there. I've never known a more caring, courageous man. And I've known a few, working on the bomb squad. Your problem is letting her go, man. She's there all right, but she ought to be in paradise waiting for her old man."

Pruett's hand went to the neck of the bottle, tears streaming down his rugged, lined features. "I can't," he said.

"You *have* to. And THAT is the first step. Oh, and in case nobody told you yet, there're a helluva lot more than twelve steps, my friend. But letting her be at peace—trust an old Injun, we're good with this kinda thing—that's what you need to do."

"This thing we're about to do, I worry about the righteousness of it all."

"Is no such thing. Righteousness is an illusion; a term made up by men and women to justify their actions. You gotta ask yourself, Jimmy, whether what you are doing is *right*. And let me tell you one last thing: *she* believes in you. You're not seeking God's approval. According to many, God flooded the entire earth to wipe away the true wretchedness."

"You believe that?"

"I believe God—just like you—would do whatever it took to protect the Good in this Universe. Whatever you got to say about the people up here—about this land and its proximity to the heavens—you know damn well what's good, and you're not only being a courageous person in the face of things most could not, you're also doing you're sworn oath. It's the whole reason you signed up, Jimmy, a moment like this. You never saw it comin', but it's here, on the doorstep of our communities, and you're doing the *good* thing. That's why she loved you."

Whitefeather stood from the railing, and put on his straw hat but he never turned back to face his friend.

"One day I will sit in that chair. It'll be a good day."

And he went to his truck and disappeared over the star-blasted horizon.

The man without a name called Pruett on Wednesday.

"You have our cash?"

"We've got a good lead. You'll get it."

"Don't make me do anything to that beautiful daughter of yours we'll both regret, mijo."

He hung up. Pruett half-grinned. Despite Pruett's admonitions, the man with no name mentioned Wendy just the same, displaying an overconfidence Pruett was counting on.

Later that day, however, the sheriff received a call he was *not* anticipating.

"Pruett," the sheriff said into his cell.

"Sheriff james Pruett. Mountain man."

It was Douglas Hale, an old friend of Pruett's who worked the DEA office out of Cheyenne. "Doug," Pruett said. "How are ya, city boy?"

"I'm going to do us both a favor of friendship and cut through the horse manure on this one, James. There's some strange information coming through southern channels that hints of a cash laundering flight that might have come up short."

"And that has to do with a no-name town way up in the Wyoming Rocky Mountains how?"

"Well, seems there's an official police report in Laramie about an alleged abduction of a young woman name of Wendy Steele. She's your daughter, I believe."

"I assure you, Doug, Wendy has nothing to do with drugs, much less a drug plane."

"Don't yank my crank and tell me it's Christmas, Pruett. We go back."

"I know we do, my friend. Love you like a brother," Pruett said. "But it's also been long enough for you to know if DEA Agent Douglas Hale needed to know something, he'd know it."

"Jimmy, this thing is aching to blow up into a full court press. A couple more pieces fall into place and Wind River's going to warrant federal investigation."

"Understood."

"Don't leave me with my dick in my hands on this, okay? All I ask."

"Wouldn't dream of it, Doug."

"I'll keep the chatter and connection of dots as minimal as I can for as long as I can. But the storm's coming. Isn't any stopping that now, brother."

"You're a good man, Douglas Hale."

"I gotta buy me a computer to do the calculations on how much you owe me."

"That's an understatement."

"Don't say shit like that. You'll get me all worked up again."

"Doug, what's happening down here, I only need another twenty-four to forty-eight hours and your organization is going to get all the appropriate calls and paperwork and everything else. NTSB, too. None of this blows back on you, I swear it."

"The NTSB. Goddammit I *knew* it. Shit. You can't promise something like that, Jimmy. But you got your two days. *IF* I can hold it all back that long. You have no idea how high this is going and how fast."

"Two days," Pruett said.

"Two."

"I'm buying the beers when you get to town."

"You're buying me a nice fucking cabin on the river where I can retire without benefits, you son of a bitch."

"Love to the missus, Doug."

Chapter 9

THE ATTACK on the Beard ranch happened at two o'clock in the morning. Just long enough for the bunkhouse crew to all finish their drink and cards and whatever other things occupied the late hours of a broken-down, unsavory group of ranch hands with the defects, lack of integrity, and inhumanity that lowered them to the point of hiring out as growers and peddlers to men like the Beards—men that had long ago degraded and devalued the honest, prideful business of ranching for a living by supplementing it first with illegal alcohol distillation, then moving to the eventual production and distribution of marijuana, and then, of course, who knew what down the line?

Team Osprey had good intel. A four-hour reconnaissance the night before had finally revealed the bags of money and three bodies—Commander Rhys Solleveld didn't have the luxury of cadaver dogs; however he was fortunate to have a buddy in the Albuquerque P.D. with a state of the art detector used for finding emissions of ninhydrin-reactive nitrogen (NRN) in its gaseous form, which is emitted by decaying corpses; the bulk of the time had been spent finding where the Beards buried those they killed. Thankfully the Beard brothers weren't much on ceremony and had dug shallow graves for Purdy, Illson, and Norman. And even more fortuitous, if not unexpected, the money was located buried near the bodies.

Osprey could have been done with it there and Pruett could have sent his deputies out the next day with a standing marijuana grower warrant and a little extra tip on the bodies but it would have then been months—even years—of trying to prove who did what killing, which ranch hands were involved, and then it wouldn't take long for someone to bring up the *cartel* drug money as leverage to reduce or eradicate prison time. Then the feds and what was planned in the Stone Creek Slough was going to be discovered.

This part of the plan made the lawman inside Pruett protest but it was the *only way* to wash the community of this blight. So Team Osprey's plan was to do more than take the cash. When the feds dropped in on this latest battle in the war on drugs, it needed the stamps of Sustantivo all over it. The cartel didn't sneak in and retrieve what was theirs.

They murdered.

They burned.

They left no life where it had teemed minutes before.

Each member of the attack team had been picked—at least in part—for their fluent Spanish spoken in the Mexican region where the cartel headquartered and operated the core of their business. They would unlikely speak, and no target would move more than a few feet, much less off the ranch, alive, but every detail had been discussed and covered. Each member also carried an M9 bayonet knife and a Soviet AK-47—both obtained from Mexican connections; both the chosen weapons of the cartel. Even the ammunition was obtained there. All evidence that remained, including the manner of death, would lead south of the border. It had to.

All but two of the team congregated outside the bunkhouse door. The other pair crept into the Beard house where both brothers were in their own rooms, well into sleeping off a solid moonshine drunk. They all flipped down the latest American-designed and manufactured night-vision micro goggles.

"*Comenzad*," whispered Osprey One and the team poured into the bunkhouse as silently as oil seeps over stone. The floor plan was simple for the bunkhouse: one large rectangular room with beds lining either side. Twelve men were hired hands for the Beards; fewer than half were any good at ranching. As the assault team worked its way into the darkened building, some of the light sleepers began waking up and the first two kills were with blades of the Mexican knives.

One man who'd spent time somewhere in the mud feigned sleep until one of the smaller female members of Osprey got close to his bunk. As he grabbed for her she easily defended his drunken, sloppy reach and said, "Luchar hasta la muerte (die hard), Americano," as she turned the AK on him and put three short bursts into his chest. The man flew backward as the force of the rounds pummeled him and stole his breath and life.

The rest of the targets began waking quickly, in various states of awareness as automatic gunfire exploded within the confined walls of the bunkhouse and the two mercenaries inside the main house, positioned for ambush, waited for the Beards to wake. They did, surprisingly quickly, stumbling from their rooms, Tom in long johns hanging halfway off his ass and Val in boxers—both shirtless, each with shotgun in hand.

Osprey Four came up behind Tom and Val somehow caught sight of the movement in the darkness.

"BROTHER."

But before Tom could react, or Val could get his shotgun raised to firing level, both assault team members had buried their knives, delivering the death coup into each brother's right kidney. A calling card of Sustantivo for the lords of opposing cartels. As was sawing off the brother's heads for display at the front of the house on green, sharpened sticks that would burn slower than the rest of the place.

The team shot whatever animals they found. They loaded all seven bags of cash in the rear of one of the SUVs and then they fueled and ignited the entire ranch: the main house, the barn, the outbuilding where the extra machinery and vehicles had a roof, and also the bunkhouse.

The night sky looked as if an entire culture had risen and built a funeral pyre for a lost, beloved king. The only property close enough to hear the gunfire and screams and to see the magnificence of the enraged flame as it roared and devoured the Beards, land and flesh, was that of the County Sheriff, sitting in his Suburban halfway down the gravel, pot-holed road to the Beards, knowing that Malcolm Whitefeather was never wrong but wanting to swallow down an entire bottle of hell just the same.

Headlights topped the horizon behind Pruett, interrupting his self-pitying moment and the hairs on his arms, neck—hell, *everywhere*—danced on end. Who would be driving up this road at nearly three in the morning? As the vehicle got closer, Pruett saw it was Mack Reynolds' beat to junk and back pickup, no doubt driven by a sloppy drunk Mack Reynolds.

When the driver saw Pruett sitting on the side of the road, the vehicle slowed down—typical drunk driver behavior—running in what the boozer thought was a straight line but looked more the shape of a spaghetti noodle thrown against the wall.

Pruett turned on his blue and red cherry toppers. He knew things were not going to end well on this one, his own hands shoved even deeper into the cookie jar.

Reynolds pulled up next to Pruett, passenger window down.

"Howdy, Shurrrriff James Q. Pruett."

"Pull over, Mack," Pruett said. "You know the drill. Put 'er in park and turn off the ignition."

Reynolds did as he was instructed. Pruett got out of the Suburban, reaching behind the seat as he did. The sheriff walked slowly up to the driver's side window, the stench of beer, whiskey, vomit, and he didn't want to know what else smacking him in the face halfway there.

"I didn't run that stop sign, did I?" the drunk said, and then howled at his own joke. "Stop sign—whew. I got a million of 'em. You know why niggers' hands and feet are white, Pruett? Oops, sorry—there a law against tellin' funny jokes?"

The sheriff had long ago gained control of his temper when it came to racist bastards like Mack Reynolds. He had to. His father and mother had to. He was pretty certain earlier generations took the front end of the insults a lot more often and in much more gruesome ways as they tried to settle their land like any other citizen.

"Ain't you gonna make me git outta the car, boy, or are you too chickenshit?"

Pruett just stood there, marveling at the fact that God could create such a worthless pile of good-for-nothingness as the drunk, racist, draft-dodging criminal before him. The animal inside him was still thirsty but this time it wasn't for booze. Just as internal pieces and parts of him had broken or malfunctioned during the war, the whole repugnant business of the cartel, the lies, the murders, and his precious daughter being taken by men without conscience or souls had done the same thing.

It was distasteful, the thing he had to do, but there was a part of him that did not regret raising the 9 MM pistol that had been obtained through Mexican channels and that he had kept in the Suburban for just such a possibility. Still, Pruett would have been lying to himself if not admitting to the exhilaration he felt running in his blood because of the fear exuding from the evil man in the truck—part of that exhilaration was the pride that he'd lived the life he had; pride that he and his ancestors had survived the small-minded, unfeeling, dangerous Mack Reynolds of the world and made Wyoming their home.

But some came from a darker place—the place where all those hateful mumblings and sluts and degradations stayed hidden behind his pride.

Reynolds was not necessarily an evil man but he was a bad one and he was a criminal; he would not be here in the middle of this situation if he weren't. He'd chosen his life, just as had a young James Pruett chosen his.

"Don't—" was all Reynolds managed to say before Pruett shot him square in the temple. The sheriff didn't figure there'd be much more mouthing off or telling of racist jokes anymore.

The blast had put the dead man flat on his back on the far side of the seat. Pruett reached in, started the engine, turned the wheels toward the barrow ditch, and put the truck's transmission in drive. The RPMs drove the truck sluggishly into the scrub and sagebrush, down one side of the ditch and up the other until it ran into a barbed-wire fence that bordered the Beard property to the south. Then the old vehicle sputtered and coughed and died, just as its owner had moments before.

Pruett walked slowly back to his Suburban and returned with a red can half-full of gasoline and emptied it inside and outside Reynolds' pickup, even dousing the open bed. He then tossed the empty plastic container in the cab and retrieved a box of wood stick matches from the shirt pocket just beneath the badge that represented the honor of the office of which he upheld.

He stepped back, lit a match, and tossed it into the cab of the truck, right on top of the body of Mack Reynolds, Pruett's face as devoid of emotion as if he'd died himself.

The next morning proved to be one of the hardest Pruett ever endured. The looks on his younger deputies were as ghosts from the past—they mirrored faces out of time; the shock, bewilderment, and awe of the new soldiers who'd just arrived in 'Nam with Pruett having seen enough devastation to be measuring time in country by years. But his deputies weren't soldiers. Yes they'd signed up, but not for this, not in a place like Wind River, Wyoming. Only Red Horse Baptiste maintained his stoic stance and went about his job.

There was no more *Beard ranch*, only if you were to compare the aftermath to Hiroshima or Nagasaki. Pruett wished the devastation were worse; that the fire had wiped more of the evidence away, not for the forensics or the land itself to make it healthier and more fertile to grow again, but rather that his young charges could not make out the burned carcasses of horses, underfed and mistreated as they had been in life.

Yes, it was a lesson they'd face one way or another in their futures but the sheriff would have to live with the fact that he'd orchestrated their meeting with the absolute and terminal cruelty of which their fellow humans were capable.

It was worse than the murder scene of Tim Mackay. The abhorrence of what had happened to that boy was understood in detail only by the sheriff and perhaps his Nez Perce deputy. At the Beard ranch the carnage was incontrovertible and appalling; there was the scorched earth as in the villages of Khe Sanh or My Lai. Those memories would live on in the intransigent way the memories of such horrors as the particular stench of charred human flesh and the sight of burnt earth and beast and human life clung to the nightmares of the witnesses. Yet all that particular dreadfulness was introduced to Pruett's deputies by *his design*.

If only he could reconcile the shame for what he'd done as the means to a necessary end—that the very lives of Deputies Munney and Canter and even Baptiste—all of Wind River and Stone Creek and the surrounding peoples—depended on each detail of this operation the way life and death lingered on each movement of the surgeon's blade, no matter how seemingly small or without import; a slight success or failure in his plan meant the difference between these young innocents waking in a few days and having life there to greet them as always or rather their town and their families and their futures scorched to the ground like the Beard ranch.

Pruett could hope to enlighten them and calm their fears, but to include them as conspirators was a far more egregious act. There were so many ways this plan could go sideways that the sheriff could not risk any of his deputies having prior knowledge or any understanding of what had taken place at the Beard ranch, why, or what would in another day commence at the Stone Creek Slough. They were innocents; they'd not signed on for a duty that called on them to mortgage their souls against the protection of a place.

That was the cross of Sheriff Pruett to put on his shoulder and carry and as he'd selflessly turned down the public display of the highest honor the Army could have awarded him, he'd do the terrible that needed doing whether altruistically or because, as he feared, God or the Devil had condemned him to be such an instrument—or harbinger—of destruction and suffering and chaos.

"We've counted all the bodies," Canter said in an understandable state of shock. "Two inside—the Beard brothers most likely b-but—"

"Zach," was all Pruett could manage.

"I never thought, I mean I-I'm sorry, Sheriff. I'm a cop. But—"

"Son, there are things none of us ever get used to, cops or no. Ask an emergency room doctor. Ask a fireman— hell, any first-responder. If we got used to it, that would make us inhuman."

It was a small lie. Or maybe not. Pruett felt used to it in a different way than he intended when speaking to young Zach Canter. What humans could or never should be able to get used to was the *capability*.

He almost smiled outwardly. How fucking contradictory could a man's conscience make him in the name of justification? HE set all this in motion. It was made to *look* as if some unimaginable monsters had perpetrated this terrible thing, but it was *his friends and comrades*. At his behest and planning. Even the brutality and utter destruction.

And there the same question for the thousandth time. *Did the end ever, EVER, justify the means?*

Perhaps only God knew. Perhaps he did not care and they were again puppets on the stage, dancing at the whim of the Grand Puppeteer.

Pruett placed his hand on Canter's shoulder. Squeezed him with iron in his will. "We'll do what we're hired to do here, Zach. The rest is for God or some other higher power than you or me. You didn't cause this. Sleep well knowing that. Sometimes it's all we'll get."

"Thanks, sir."

"Go on with your report, son."

"Three bodies behind the house, twenty meters. One is identifiable as Reb Norman. Assumption would be that makes the other two, Purdy, and Illson, but the coroner will need dental records. Same for the eleven bodies where the bunkhouse used to be. The twelfth ranch hand we figure is Mack Reynolds; that's his burned out truck we saw coming in."

"Guess Shriver lucked out, being kin and probably part of the conspiracy. Good work, Deputy. You'll make a fine sheriff one day."

"Not sure I want to," said Canter. "No offense, sir."

"None taken."

The sheriff and his team continued the forensics, picking up shell casings Pruett knew would trace back to ammunition purchased in Juarez and that had been fired by eastern bloc AK-47s that would eventually be found to have been supplied to the cartel by United States entities—news reports for months had been running that claimed the Mexican cartels may have been armed as much as eighty-five percent by organizations in the United States.

Coroner Scoot Morgan and, later, the federal Medical Examiners, would find the knife wounds on those bodies where they could be measured would match the M9 bayonet knives used by the cartel.

There were no survivors to contradict the story and Pruett worried that the next night's exchange would come too late for the feds to drop into his necessary but illegal machinations. It would have to be enough time; there certainly wasn't enough left to change things now. Wendy would be dead and the town desecrated if Pruett and his army of pioneer residents or the Osprey team that would be their backup could not successfully subdue the men the cartel sent to get the drug money.

Again the plan relied on underestimation and Pruett knew damn well he'd bet on that horse more than once too often.

Chapter 10

OMAR AND his two accomplices drove the three hundred miles of deadpan, sagebrush, and the occasional butte or mountain peak breaking the horizon between Laramie and Wind River.

"This country, she is flatter than your home," he said to Wendy, who was gagged and bound in the second row of seats in the black Hummer with windows tinted so dark nothing could be seen from the outside.

Wendy made no sound, nor did she register any movement to acknowledge she'd heard a word said. She'd barely spoken since her abduction, in part because she had no idea in the world what was going on. Who the people were who'd taken her and of what they were capable was fairly clear. Beyond that, and some deal being brokered by her father—the sheriff of a town that most people had never heard of—she knew *nothing*. So she planned on saying nothing.

Omar would wait for his instructions as to the exchange place for the money. His instructions were clear, as always: neither the woman, the sheriff, nor any other people at the meeting location were to walk away alive. No pain or torture or cartel signatures; none beyond clean, professional kills.

No witnesses. Leaving witnesses was sloppy and the cartel was nothing if not elegant with their attention to each detail. Also, someone other than a few idiotic twentysomethings with a combined Intelligence Quotient of an orangutan had to be shown to have paid a price for the stolen money.

The sheriff and his daughter would be enough of a message, of this his boss had assured him and of course, Cristóbal had ordered *him*.

Omar and the pock-faced man with no name had not yet heard of the attack on the Beard ranch. How the sheriff acquired the money was of no concern or consequence to the cartel's mission. And Omar's boss was clear on another matter: if the sheriff came up short, Omar *would* remove a piece of his cherished daughter. There were details that were always followed; exceptions were rare or nonexistent.

"We have the money," Pruett spoke into the phone receiver. His stomach twisted and flipped inside like a cobra dancing to the piper. He'd not stopped thinking about his daughter for hours. He'd sat in his cabin and gone through every old picture he owned. It was his only way toward the strengthening of resolve.

"This is good news, compadre."

"I'm no *compadre* of yours, sir. Don't be fucking insulting."

"I don't mind saying, Sheriff, I wouldn't mind an hour alone with you. Bare hand to bare hand. Mano a mano."

"We may have just agreed for the first time," Pruett said.

"I could introduce myself properly."

"Says you."

"Where to exchange the bags for your lovely daughter?"

"Stone Creek Slough."

"What is this *sloo*?"

"It's a bridge just off the main highway. You know where Stone Creek is?"

"Twelve to thirteen clicks southern, from your town of Wind River," the man with no name said.

"Yes. The slough is where the old main bridge still sits— when they repaved the highway they rebuilt the bridge to make it more modern, safer for today's larger vehicles. They left the old bridge in place because the ranchers can still use it and avoid bringing their equipment on to the main highway. It's perfect; the bridge is not noticeable from the highway, particularly around dusk. I suggest we meet on the bridge, one car each. We can then each back out the way we came."

"Hmm, I'd like to see this bridge first."

"You set the timetable," Pruett said. "I've busted my ass to find and retrieve your money and to get this exchange set up without my whole crew finding out has been hard enough. I picked this location for its simplicity as well as its covertness. I don't have any room left to be considering further options."

"Tonight, then, at your *sloo*. The woman for the money."

"You don't want the directions?"

"I know the bridge of which you speak. Seven P.M. We will come down the road from the north, you the south. If you break your word, you lose your baby girl, and we will have our money one way or the other."

"Understood," said Pruett, though he knew the former would never happen, not in the eyes of the murderer who'd just agreed to the final phase of Pruett's wild plan. The man with no name—the psycho son of a bitch—loved the location better than Pruett himself. No better place to kill a sheriff, his daughter, take the money, and leave for the south, unseen, and undetected.

The sheriff immediately called Solleveld. "We're a go for tonight."

"Señor Cristóbal," said the pockmarked man. "The transfer of money is tonight, where we planned. The surrounding ridges will provide excellent cover for the backup men. I have two vans with over a dozen Sustantivo soldiers each—one parked south five miles of Stone Creek and the bridge, one parked north. A single man from each van will blockade the highway from both directions. There is a third van with a dozen more."

"*Excelente*," said his boss. "Afterward you burn everything. We've never made such a mark on small claim territory before, compadre—we want this to resonate for decades. Big city, small town, Sustantivo shall not be taken lightly anywhere in the world."

"Si, jefe."

"You have enough men?"

"The sheriff, he talk tough—and he is; a man of our caliber even, perhaps—but he is alone here, a rooster amongst a coop of chickens."

"Do not fail me."

"No, jefe. All will be done as you wish."

Wendy's hood had been removed shortly after her abduction from the apartment and the SUV was on the Interstate, as if she could not tell the directions in her own state. But that was not it. The hood was unnecessary for captives that would not live. As the driver took them north from Rock Springs on Highway 191 she thought about the end. She wondered if she'd see her father again—if he were even still alive.

So much grief over the years. Since the loss of her mother, though, it had seemed as if life might reshuffle and give Wendy and her father a better hand. For three years it had been so. Now, out of the blue, she was being driven to her own execution.

For what? She wanted to ask a hundred questions but refused to give her captors the satisfaction of her curiosity, her fear, her confusion, or even her attention. Such presence of evil in the world made all the things she hated necessary: war, hate, suspicion, and mistrust—the distance between humans that grew exponentially every year.

All the horrors sensationalized on twenty-four hour news channels yet here she was, in the middle of the drama, wondering if the reporting were exaggerated at all. If a woman could be considering a marriage proposal one moment and the next be stolen away and transported to (she could only assume) her hometown to die, could such an anti-humanitarian stance be justified? Should the inhabitants of the world find their cabins or their caves and shut themselves away from the horrors of the world— terrifying acts carried out every minute of every day by their fellow human beings?

Wendy had travelled the world with the Peace Corps and saw the brutality of the death squads and the unnecessarily thirsty and starving children, their torsos like ribbed shells containing their hope and sadness, pressed together by their thirst and famine. First arrivers often mistook the expressions on the native's faces as genuine gladness that help had arrived, but it soon enough became clear that cheerfulness was pretended and disillusionment was the only thing the starving understood or believed.

Had she been cocooned in her own disillusionment—the apathy of small town American living, law school, being in love—that she'd forgotten the horrors of eighty percent of the rest of the planet?

Apparently she was about to be reminded.

Pruett had only a few hours to finish his work. He placed Deputy Baptiste in charge of assisting Scoot and getting the bodies into the Coroner's wagon and on toward the morgue where he could begin his autopsies. He gave a standing order that *all* external communications—particular those *federal* in nature—were to be directed to him personally and that he was not reachable until the next day.

In the weeks to follow, after the federal buzzards had plucked and picked at the Black Jack Ranch crime scene to their satisfaction, he would get the County Commissioners to hire the County Shop to bulldoze the entire gruesome acreage. Until then, those bastards could all smolder—for eternity, Pruett hoped.

Whitefeather met him at the Stone Creek Community Center around one o'clock, where a few of the key members of the local ranch community were to be in another hour or so.

"Hard to imagine that seven duffel bags full of cash could bring about such Armageddon," Whitefeather said, staring at the black bags.

"Is it?" said Pruett.

"Not really. Just seemed like the appropriate thing to say."

"I'm thinking you might ought to sit this one out," said the sheriff.

"You thinkin' about retirin' to Vietnam, too? Go fuck yourself. I've earned my place tonight as much as you."

"That's not what I meant and you know it."

"Well sentimentality is *not* what we need at this present position where we've dug in."

"All right then," Pruett said. "You want to hear the rest of the details now?"

The old Blackfoot gave him a look to un-stink shit.

"Okay, okay—you know how crazy it's been. I'm not holding out on ya."

"Talk."

"When Jensen, Pape, Grassell, and Lauger get here, we'll go over it again, so forgive me if I present the highlights."

"More'n I have so far," said Whitefeather.

"Each of the four men have twenty or more men with rifles—they'll come at the ridges from all directions, waiting for Wendy to emerge from the vehicle before surrounding the Mexicans. All in we should have over a hundred marksmen to bear down on our targets."

"Men?"

"A few women, too," said Pruett.

"You realize their vehicle—assuming there's only one— will be armored."

"Rhys has provided a healthy number of weapons for the more experienced locals with armor-piercing rounds."

"And?"

"Some new explosive devices."

"See, I told you I was necessary."

"A necessary evil, I'd say."

"Like you aren't."

"The key is getting Wendy clear. I figure we meet halfway, where we've got the bags of money. I'll ask to have her alive first—a good faith gesture—but he won't agree to it," Pruett said.

"And then?"

"Rhys's the best sniper I know. I engaged him because it's the only way I can figure to ensure we drop whoever's got Wendy. I'll grab her and get her safely behind the Suburban."

"That's your plan?"

"Well there has to be some point where you go on instinct—can't plan every detail."

"Who's there with you?"

"Just me, that's how they want it; a simple exchange."

"And two dead Pruetts. I'm going down there with you. He's not going to be alone."

"I know he isn't—that's what Rhys is there for, Mal. I saw him take down four NVA regulars without drawing a single breath."

"I'm talking inside the vehicle. I'd be shocked if you don't get at least three of those, too, by the way. What about your deputies?"

"I won't ask them to be a part of this. Not young law enforcement officers. Melody and Zach are barely past being kids themselves. Has to be someone around this town that hasn't seen the shit you and I have seen; done what we've had to do."

"You don't think they'd want to be next to their sheriff, protecting their town, like the rest of the folk that'll be here? You deprive them of that chance, you're keepin' 'em on the outside, not protectin' 'em."

"Think I don't know that, do ya? It's my choice and I made it. When the DEA and NTSB and whoever else starts poking around with their questions—"

"And if there needs to be a fall guy," Whitefeather said, "you'll be him."

"Damn right I will. I won't chance their careers."

"And Baptiste?"

"He'll be here. His family owes some kind of blood oath to mine. He'd kill me if I didn't have him up here."

"Then that gives us three," Whitefeather said. "When Rhys drops 'em, you get your gun out and be ready to start shootin'. Baptiste, too. I'll grab Wendy and get her to safe ground. By the time the shooting starts, you won't hold the locals back. That's going to become one hot fire zone."

"It's getting harder and harder to keep my mind around this thing, Mal. The whole Wendy piece—it's got me thirsting something fierce. Like my head is getting muddier and sloppier each day, when I can least afford it."

"S'why I'm here, chief. To keep you on the straight and narrow."

Kale Jensen came through the doors of the Community Center. "Sheriff," he said, touching the brim of his Stetson. Then he looked at Malcolm. "Mr. Whitefeather," he said.

"Call me Mal, son."

"Yessir. The other guys are runnin' a couple minutes late, but they'll be here. Grassell said something about seeing a guy about a dog."

The two old gents smiled.

Two seconds later the door busted open and Ty McIntyre roared into the room, marched over to Pruett as if he were going to tear him apart, then stopped with his chiseled, whiskered face just inches from the sheriff's.

"You think you can keep me outta this fray, Sheriff? After what we've been through together?"

"Easy, Ty. I figured you paid your debt, and then some. Just trying to leave you in peace."

"Now that Bethy's gone, we're brothers. Real ones. Her dyin' solidified that and you know it. Why you'd consider savin' my niece without me—y'all think I couldn't be useful?"

Ty then threw his arms around Pruett and about squeezed the life from him.

"You sober?" Pruett said after the hug.

"As a church mouse."

Pruett turned to Whitefeather. "Looks like you have your fourth. Ty, when the shooting starts, you wrangle up Wendy get her the fuck outta Dodge."

McIntyre nodded.

"Place is going to go off like the Fourth a July about then, I expect, so you don't stop until she's out of harm's way," Pruett said. "I have a better idea for you, Mal."

"Don't need no help from no Injun anyway," Ty said. "Can save my niece my own self."

Chapter 11

THE MEETING with Rhys Solleveld was the final instrumental piece to Sheriff Pruett's master orchestration. However, he'd kept Solleveld's involvement in their second event from his best friend, Malcolm Whitefeather. The Osprey Insertion Team was, as far as Whitefeather knew—and more importantly, as far as the cartel would ever know—a strictly secondary option; to Whitefeather's knowledge it was only a failsafe in the case of a complete breakdown in Plan A.

Pruett knew better. The cartel would come at him stronger than they said, harder than he wanted, and—like him—would be intent on leaving a signature message behind after their passage. That meant more vehicles, more men, and a whole different battle plan than he'd originally laid out for the residents of Stone Creek. If the session of planning with Commander Solleveld went as hoped, they could construct reinforcement into Plan A rather than changing any element of it.

The two soldiers met at the Wooden Boot saloon and sat in the back. It didn't matter all that much; everyone sat in the shadows at the Wooden Boot.

"So I've been going over this all day, James," said Solleveld.

"And?"

"I like your thoughts about augmenting your *Plan A*, but you knew I would be asking for more involvement from the get-go."

"And I knew we'd need it," said Pruett. "My concern—as you know—is that we make this stand. The locals."

"If hired soldiers kill a contingent of cartel men, it's an everyday battle."

"Exactly. I want these bastards to know what kind of resolve we have—heaven knows we don't have the artillery to stop them if they really wanted to own all of Wyoming. Ain't trying to send that message. But they won't play fair, and my only hole card to keep the game honest is you and your people."

Solleveld laid out a map of the Stone Creek area, focusing on the land horseshoeing the slough and ending on the high ridgelines Pruett intended for his armed cavalry. "What you figure, James, two or three vehicles on the bridge plus yours?"

"Let's plan for three."

"Standard three by two, then, we'll call it six per vehicle minus one being your daughter. So seventeen targets but we concentrate on vehicle number one—or whichever produces your girl. Five primary targets, your nameless man my prime objective."

Not that Rhys Solleveld would have any trouble with the whole lot of them, much less five men around his daughter. He was the best sniper Pruett had ever heard of.

"Cutting to the chase, as you know me to do, I'm not worried too much about your taking out the contingency."

"Right. I figure they're planning for the same high ground as you. Only thing that makes mil'try sense. I figure you hold back your people until my team eliminates whomever they send to the ridgelines. Silent kills; your element of surprise intact, mate."

"So you've seen—the plan is, the nameless bastard drops, and as the others begin to follow suit, Ty McIntyre—Wendy's tough as turpentine uncle—grabs her up and hustles her outta there. He'll keep her shielded. Tried to talk him into a vest; he wouldn't even let me get all the words out. Bull rider. That's all I have to say about that."

Rhys smiled.

"Whitefeather has cooked up some claymores on steroids for the vehicles and underneath the bridge. I stay until he's done; the last to go, there's no arguing that."

"Then we disagree. You and your daughter represent high profile targets to the cartel. They'll be counting you as coups; top of their own list."

"Whitefeather goes, I go. That's how it works. Don't give me some nonsense about how it's different for you. You get it five-by-five, so move on."

"It's why I've always loved you, James, from the first moment we ate together in that mess tent."

Solleveld always made 'James' sound like he was talking about a chauffer or special servant to the Queen. "Well you don't disagree with me, do ya?"

"No. Last man out. Captain with his ship and all that bloody malarkey."

"Good Christ, man, you Brits need to update your language to the twentieth century one day."

"The day we bastardize English the way you blokes here have is the day I put a bullet in my brain," Solleveld said, smiling wryly. "Same thing with beer."

"Hail the revolution," said Pruett.

"And a polite 'fuck you' to you, Sir James."

Pruett checked his watch. Four more hours. He'd already talked to the four group leaders of the ranchers. Told them to let Osprey do their thing and then Plan A as always, just a little later than planned.

His cell rang. Whitefeather calling.

"Pruett."

"Whitefeather."

Then silence.

"What you call for, Mal?"

"Oh geeze, sorry—thought we was just sharin' last names. Secret code or somethin'."

"Thanks for the smile," Pruett said, and meant it. He was sweating, thirsting from every duct on his person, and having heart palpitations. He was pretty certain there was nothing in his job description as sheriff about military-style battle with a drug cartel.

"Thanks for keeping me in the dark," Whitefeather spat.

"Solleveld."

"You think soldiers keep secrets from other soldiers?"

"No, I think friends do what they think's best for friends. Not the same thing, chief—apples to oranges."

"Fuck you very much. A, I ain't never been a Chief. B, I'm a soldier—friend first other days, soldier first today."

"Fair enough. Rhys tell you the basics?"

"Damn right he did. What's this last man out horse puckey?

"It's non-negotiable for one thing."

"You ain't the Captain. There ain't no ship."

"This is my doing—this is going down on my watch, my plan, and if you make me pull rank soldier, *I'm* the sheriff."

"I ain't deputized. And I pay my taxes, so that kinda makes me *your* boss."

"Look," Pruett said. "We go together."

"Huh-uh. You're a primary target. I'm an old Injun; they'll probably think I wandered onto the scene."

"They know who you are and that you're a lot smarter and more dangerous to them collectively than I ever could be."

"Now you're just sweet-talking me."

"You need to reach the top first to trigger the claymores."

"Not just *claymores*. Whitefeather claymores. Much more bang, velocity, and spread for the buck."

"And the trigger?"

"We go TOGETHER. Ain't leaving you behind, brother."

"Then we finally agree," said Pruett, sweating for a double Heaven Hill.

Chapter 12

THE GLOAMING light was settling on the landscape; the revitalizing smell of a forthcoming rain impended, the dark purple clouds gathered around the Rocky Mountains having begun to move down toward Wind River and the Stone Creek valley. A lone osprey soared on the then calm wind currents, near translucent in flight against the low light, the dark-colored markings underneath creating a skeletal appearance.

Earlier in the day the Wyoming sky was so blue it looked canvas-painted with a scattering of white clouds as insignificant as lost balls of cotton. With the progression of the day, however, the thunderheads had grown and surrounded the mountain peaks, firing bolts of lightning as if Zeus himself were warring with the Wind Rivers.

Pruett, at the top of the road leading down to Stone Creek Bridge, checked his watch. 6 P.M. The rain might arrive before the meeting time but that would be an advantage for Rhys and his team; their training was always in the worst of conditions. Although the rain shower might pass over or drop a lighter load, the clouds looked portentous and Pruett was stressed, trying to anticipate all the angles, particularly any that offered them an advantage. Consequently his desire for a drink had never plagued him more egregiously—the eternal succubus of his soul, demanding her insatiable gorge.

Malcolm Whitefeather waited in the passenger seat of the Suburban, still studying his small, home-tweaked mines. Not that there was much to be done about them now; he was mostly concerned with the remote trigger device and its communication UHF signal with the puck-sized explosives.

Ty McIntyre, who they'd picked up last since he lived in Stone Creek, sat in the rear. He was sober as Sunday, didn't want to talk, and had only wanted to know his part in saving Wendy's life. That he swore to Pruett he'd accomplish or die first.

Pruett glanced in the mirror and marveled at the flat, detached, determined set of his marbled eyes. Many times Pruett had figured Ty a man who was better seen on the other side of the street and the sheriff could attest to the old cowpoke's barbaric strength and rattlesnake quickness and dexterity, but in the leathered countenance reflected back to him he realized there was no other he'd rather have on Wendy's behalf that night.

At 6:30 PM, Pruett put the old Suburban into gear, drove down to the bridge, and edged the vehicle until it was occupying just the southernmost end, leaving room to the north for the multiple armored SUVs he and Rhys agreed were likely coming.

Rhys and his team were above, in the scrub and sagebrush, awaiting the expected cartel contingency. How many men were coming they could not know, but Team Osprey's twenty-five could conservatively handle five times that many soldiers—fighters mediocrely-trained at best—and that would be a conservative estimate, Pruett knew. Osprey's strategy was one of placement; the residents of Stone Creek, Wind River, and other parts of the state were to wait until Rhys' team had finished their work and then would approach from behind the established skirmish line.

Whitefeather got out of the Suburban and opened the back of the truck.

"What the fuck's *he* doin'?" Ty said.

"Mal is an explosives expert. Part of the plan requires his expertise," Pruett said.

"Holy shit. You make sure I git Wendy clear and that old Injun don't pull the trigger 'til yer safe, Pruett. I told you, now, we're brothers."

"You didn't care much for your brothers," Pruett said. "As I recall for damn good reason."

"That's why I need to keep safe a good one."

Pruett smiled. Ty was a likable man at his core, despite the truculent, barbed, crab-shell exterior of the man himself.

Pruett turned. "Come on. Let's unload that money. Can't stand the stench anymore."

"Me neither," Ty said. "Let's do 'er."

The prairie encircled the ridgeline of the slough in a bit of a horseshoe configuration, so Rhys had his team divided into thirds and waiting for the cartel. The rain arrived first. It started as a few engorged drops but within a minute or two teemed down from above like a tropical torrent; water began to run in muddy rivers through the sage almost immediately—where it was dry moments before it was, instantly, ankle-deep.

Team Osprey was happy for the change in weather as they'd already dressed for it and all weapons and gear were previously waterproofed. And when the cartel vehicles arrived around eighteen-fifteen military time (6:15 P.M.)— three vans from three different spots over the horizon, barreling over the landscape at ridiculous speeds—the rain provided excellent cover from a distance.

(Rhys actually believed this one of the most dangerous moments for his team as they were committed to exact, second-by-second communication of the cartel vehicles' locations so that a member of the insertion team did not find themselves beneath the crushing weight of a moving vehicle, so well-hidden were his squad.)

The strategy was for the commandos to move along the directional tangents of the vehicles, also having preplanned the approximate locations they would choose to stop, and attempt to reach them as they began disembarking. The team would engage their opponents in three congregated groups rather than give them the opportunity to disperse and require a more open-field, wide-angled assault.

Rhys had anticipated the plans of the cartel well enough that by the time the thirty-some cartel soldiers in their three approaching vehicles stopped and exited their vans, eight members of Team Osprey had them surrounded in a half-circle spread with each van.

The cartel soldiers—more afraid of failing their bosses and of their own considerable pride than death—did not intend on being beaten or captured. Three short firefights, drowned out both by the silencers in use and the raging storm, were over very quickly.

Rhys' team sustained one field-containable injury and the thirty-some cartel members all died serving their masters. And as if on cue the Wyoming weather—which as a rule turns in a moment, anyway—began to subside, the blood of the battle running away with the last of the water, soaking into the voraciously thirsty and unforgiving soil.

The cartel's contingency now eliminated in whole, three members of Rhys' team jogged back across the prairies and scrub to bring the rancher army forward to the ridgeline, the time then only twenty-five minutes before the scheduled meeting on the bridge. Rhys himself was running short on time to get himself into position.

Eighty-four-year-old "Long-Pole" LaRue Hilton, who had survived and healed from his courtroom battle three years earlier, was driving his battered, '66 Dodge pickup northbound on Highway 191, just five miles or so south of Stone Creek when he saw the construction roadblock up ahead. There were cones covering both lanes and a Hispanic man in a reflective yellow vest waving for him to stop. LaRue noticed no vehicle parked that would have gotten the man to this place in the road so close to sundown, but neither would the construction worker have noticed that the Remington 1889 side-by-side 10-gauge shotgun LaRue inherited from his father and always carried in his gun rack was missing from its perch.

LaRue slowed down, nice and easy, and came to a stop, putting the old Dodge in park but leaving the engine running. The rotund Hispanic man smiled and walked up to the window LaRue was just rolling down.

"No can go this way," the stranger said, his accent thick and hard on his English.

"No can go?" LaRue said. "Why the fuck not? My home's up yonder."

"Road hurt. Damage," the man said.

"Hurt, huh?" LaRue said. "Wanna know what pisses me off? Outsiders thinkin' they can just come to anybody's town and push 'em around."

The stranger looked confused, as if he'd been told no one would question him. It was also clear he struggled to find a response in *Ingles*.

"You go back," was all the man in the bright yellow vest could muster. He never saw the side-by-side barrels slide out from beneath Long-pole LaRue's coat, resting on the windowsill and pointed straight at his chest, nor the two cocked hammers on the reliable old gun.

"No, hombre, *you go*," said the old rancher and released both hammers. The 10-gauge sounded like a cannon when both shells went off simultaneously and the man in the reflective yellow exploded in a cloud of red and flew backward ten yards. He did not get up again, and LaRue reloaded his shotgun, put it on the rack in his window, and maneuvered around the traffic cones. Half a mile down the highway he took an old ranch road that would bring him out north of the other roadblock, where he would greet the other construction worker.

Only two Sustantivo SUVs—a pair of Hummers, the glass tinted black and probably bulletproof and the steel of which they were constructed was clearly high-grade protective. They drove down the road and stopped only a yard apart at the far northern end of the bridge. All doors opened though only the man with no name and the driver stepped out of the first vehicle. The pockmarked man pointed to the bags lying ten feet in front of Pruett's Suburban and said, very loudly: "You have left us the longer walk, Sheriff."

Pruett answered: "Where is my daughter?"

"She is here, in my vehicle. Omar guards her; he keeps her safe."

"I want to see her and speak with her."

The no-name man paused as if in thought and then waved. Omar stepped out of the first cartel SUV and gently helped Wendy from the second row seating. She looked fine but Ty, still inside the sheriff's vehicle, said, "I'll kill every one of them sons a bitches," when he saw his niece for the first time.

Pruett waved behind him in a shushing motion.

"You came with more than just yourself, Sheriff."

"Said the man with no name and two armored vehicles full of men," said Pruett.

"Si, si. *Me parece justo.* Fair enough, Sheriff Pruett. Hch. Fair enough. I bring extra men only to carry the bags of money, but you make an *excelente* point."

"Can we just get on with the exchange? You have my *daughter*, sir. I see this as no time for fucking around or playing games. Your money is all there—I'll even wait until you count it—but may I have my baby girl back now, please."

"We meet at the money. Your daughter, she is the most important thing to you. The money is to me."

Thank God, Pruett thought. And then the doors on the second SUV all opened. Pruett instinctively placed his hand on his holster, as if it would have done him any good. The pockmarked man held up his palms to the air in a gesture of disarmament.

"Please, Sheriff, for the money only. Unarmed, I assure you."

"Keep 'em in the vehicle until after the exchange," Pruett said. "Then I don't care. No sooner. *No sooner.* Comprende?"

"Si, after exchange. Your passengers remain, too?"

"My relative Ty will come to take Wendy back so that I can stay with you until the money is counted, loaded, whatever. That way you still have me—an assurance."

The man nodded. "And the other?"

"An old friend of mine. Moral support—I couldn't get him to stay home. He's of no consequence or worry to you."

Whitefeather scowled behind the darkening windshield.

"Okay," the boss said and motioned to the man called Omar to come around.

Cocky bastard. Figures any minute the cavalry comes over the rise and us country bumpkins are square outta luck, Pruett thought.

Whitefeather's door was already open, as was Ty's. Ty got out while the sheriff took off his holster and laid his weapon on the hood of the Suburban. Omar brought Wendy forward, her hands still tied in front, her face a veneer of dread. Both Omar and the pockmarked man removed weapons and placed them on their Hummer.

The two groups—Ty and Pruett; the no-name man, Omar, and Wendy—slowly walked toward the pile of cash-filled bags. Wendy's eyes remained locked on her father's and as the two got near enough for her to see the emotion and terror unsuccessfully hidden deep within his, she started to cry.

"Not now, baby girl. There'll be time."

Pruett noticed both Omar and the nameless man's eyes flitting, looking up, a complexion of confusion growing slightly on their faces. Soon they had all stopped on alternate sides of the stack of duffels, they and the bridge's surface soaked from the earlier downpour. Muddy water spidered away in a variety of rivulets, streams, and the bridge was covered in muddy puddles.

Omar looked down at the bags first. "There are seven."

"Observant cuss," said Ty, flashing his wooden hangman's smile.

"Shut up, Ty," Pruett said. "Seven. That's all of them."

"There were eight," the man with no name said flatly.

"There was also a plane crash," Pruett said. "Seven is all there ever were."

"Seven, eight, this is all irrelevant," said the nameless man. He extended his hand to Pruett. "My name is Enrique."

Pruett stared. His diplomacy didn't fail him. His memory served—message received. Yet before he could answer or Omar could remove the knife he'd brought with him, the setting sun broke through the still pregnant clouds, just clearing the ridgeline to the west and cast the shadows of at least a hundred bodies on the muddied bridge.

Everyone instinctually looked upward and the sight became a framed artwork in Pruett's head. Dozens and dozens of locals circling the small contingent of people below on the bridge. Not cartel men.

Proud Wyoming people.

Armed Wyoming people.

Even with the cartel's extra vehicle they were outnumbered ten to one.

Each person on the ridge held a rifle and they were all pointed down from that elevated perch.

"You'll never make it back to the trucks," Pruett said.

"You and your daughter will never see another sunrise," said Enrique, and he reached behind, into his belt, and all the action slowed in Pruett's mind.

Before Pruett could react, Enrique had his pistol pointed at Wendy's head.

The gun, however, dropped from his hand as a round hole in his head appeared and the man who now had a name fell in a heap of lifelessness.

Ty lunged for Wendy just as Omar's knife cleared its sheath, however the old cowpoke stumbled over the huge pile of money bags and decided at the last moment to roll his momentum into Omar instead, tackling him, rolling him, and flinging the knife free as it tumbled through the air.

By then men had poured out of the vehicles, each with two orders in mind: kill the woman and the sheriff.

Rifle fire erupted from the ridge and cartel men began to drop, one after the other. Those few that survived the first volley from the ridge began to panic and scatter.

Except one.

Wendy froze, unsure of which way to run; the pile of bags and the wrestling match going on between Ty and Omar blocked Pruett.

There were still over a dozen armed cartel men and Pruett saw one charging them at full tilt level his gun at Wendy, who was still not moving a muscle. Before the man could fire, however, Wendy was airborne—flying like a bird.

Rhys Solleveld had sprung up from a break in the bridge, where he'd been hiding in the undercarriage ironwork, and had her in a fireman's carry rushing her to safety.

A half second later the sniper dropped the charging man and the scene became a free-fire zone. Some of the four or five remaining cartel employees, for fear of their lives, returned fire at the ranchers above and died. Two returned to an armor-plated vehicle and other ranchers armed with Rhys' guns and piercing ammunition began taking the SUV apart.

Pruett couldn't run—Ty was beginning to lose his battle with Omar, the trained killer. The sheriff looked back but his holster was too far behind him, so he scooped up

Enrique's sidearm and climbed across the bags, placing the muzzle against Omar's head.

"STOP OR DIE."

Omar immediately desisted and Ty rolled over to where the knife lay.

"Gonna cut you stem ta stern you Mexican bast—"

Pruett stepped in his way, the gun still trained on Omar.

"Get back to the top, Ty," Pruett said. "Make sure my baby girl is all right."

"You kill that sonofabitch, Pruett, or I *will*."

"Ty, you're my brother now. And I'm asking you to listen to me and do this—for Bethy, if that's what it takes. *Please go.*"

The cowboy stood there, jaw agape for just a moment, and then he turned and took off toward his niece who was already far from the slough.

"Put your hands on your head," Pruett told Omar, who was now kneeling. Omar complied.

Malcolm Whitefeather came running up and said, "Holy shit, boss, that was like Khe Sanh or somethin' for about two or three minutes."

"You know what to do now," Pruett said, drained, angry, *done.*

Whitefeather nodded and ran forward amongst the strewn cartel bodies.

"I learned something interesting in my investigation," Pruett said to Omar.

"Which is?"

"Among other things, you are Cristóbal Casales' cousin."

"On his father's side," Omar said.

"Turn around, keeping your hands where they are. Stay kneeling."

Omar did as he was told and whispered a Catholic prayer in Spanish.

Pruett pulled out the steel and handcuffed Omar, right hand, then left.

"We don't go in for blood feuds in this territory. You live to tell of what you saw here."

Whitefeather wired the SUVs and the bags of money. Because he had more time than anticipated, he added some accelerants and other chemicals for a very nice show. Tough to beat any fireworks where you know twenty-million dollars is going up in flames. The ranchers cheered as the drug money burst into an all-consuming fire, burned to the last dollar.

"Cristóbal will kill you all for that," Omar told Pruett quietly, so no one else could hear.

Pruett leaned in close to Omar's ear and said, "But he'll think twice."

All the ranchers, Rhys, his team, Pruett, Wendy, and Omar stayed gathered on the ridge to wait for Malcolm Whitefeather to pull the trigger on his real masterpiece. The scene took on the look of the movie *Apocalypse Now* and made Pruett wonder how any living thing survived that war.

Both SUVs blew twenty feet in the air and *then* burst into a thousand pieces from a secondary device. There was enough incendiary material placed beneath the bridge to eradicate the bridge, remaining vehicle parts, cartel bodies, and left a crater in the earth so large the roads both north and south were obliterated as was the landscape for fifty yards in all directions (and this with Whitefeather designing the bulk force of the blast in a straight up direction).

"Nice work, Mal. There's no one in the business like you."

"What are you going to do with *him*," Whitefeather said, indicating Omar.

"He's a blood relative of the owners of Sustantivo. I'm banking that this gesture of life won't go unnoticed."

"And if it does?"

"Then we may get another visit," Pruett said.

"People tend to take twenty-some million dollars pretty personally, you know."

"That is exactly what I told him," Omar said.

"You shut yer mouth when yer talkin' to me," said Whitefeather. "Wouldn't lower myself to speak to ya much less *agree* with ya."

Pruett walked his friend out of earshot of Omar.

"In the tradition of the Casales family—better said, of the region in which the generations of their family grew up—nothing is more sacred than blood or the land," Pruett said.

"Like the Blackfeet."

"Yes."

"Like the people up here in Wyoming."

"*Yes.*"

"Well that's all you had to tell me," said Whitefeather.

"I did tell you that."

"How you going to get your little pet back to its owner?"

Pruett smiled. "Having him delivered on the Rhys Express."

"Another message?"

"Some might call it that," Pruett said.

"You can reach me here, I can reach you there," said Whitefeather.

"If so interpreted."

Chapter 13

RACHEL SHEPARD was admitted to the Jackson Hole St. John's Medical Center after Pruett's team found her the day after what the sheriff considered the Stone Creek Massacre but was being reported to the DEA officially as two rival cartels battling for the same product and/or money with one side's explosives going off a bit too soon and unexpectedly.

A few days later, Pruett learned that she was awake and coherent and he drove up to visit her in her room. When he arrived he laid the bouquet of creamy yellow daisies on her bed table and asked if he could close the door and sit with her a while.

Rachel nodded but did not smile. Her face was still swollen and the multiple bruises did not look fresh and purple. They had turned a raven, sallow, almost sulfurous yellow, like that of a jaundiced, overripe lemon.

The rape kit report had been given to the sheriff and indicated massive trauma to her genitals, anal cavity, and throat. She'd also been severely beaten about seventy percent of her body, one arm and her nose broken, and three ribs cracked, all of it making Pruett sorry he'd even considered letting Omar go free.

Pruett dragged the tall-back hospital chair over close to the bed and the faux leather crackled and groaned as Pruett sat down. "I'll try to do most of the talking so you can simply rest, child," he said.

Rachel did not nod but closed her eyes and a single tear ran the length of her left cheek and dripped off her chin onto the bed linens.

Pruett kept his voice low and pleasant. "We're aware of most details," he said. "You're not in any trouble, Rachel, I wanted you to know that first and foremost. I'm here more as a friend than anything else. I wanted to come. This is not an interview. I just wanted to say a few things to you that I feel might help you in the days to come. Is that all right?"

She nodded, just barely perceptibly.

"You don't know me well, Rachel, but I tend to speak my mind, so please, just give me the signal if you'd care for me to stop. I've been through some traumatic things in my life. Most I never want to talk about with anyone, not ever again. But if I knew then what I know now, I would talk to a professional in a heartbeat, honey. A *heartbeat*. It's confidential, whatever you say, and it does help, I swear it on my wife, Rachel. It will help you cope. That's all I'll say on that matter.

"This is going to feel like it was your fault, if it doesn't already, and that's normal. Normal doesn't make it true. It's not true, Rachel. I've done ten dozen things in my early days but for one turn or another could've turned out terrible for me, my friends, and even strangers we didn't know. I have to admit to you—setting aside my oath as sheriff—if I was younger, I think I might've done the same thing. I would have thought about it as pennies from Heaven, child. I swear it."

Tears ran down Rachel's discolored, distended skin, her eyes still closed tightly.

"It's true. Who can predict such outcomes? Not me, not you, not *anyone*."

"Tim died," she said in a garbled attempt at clean speech. Pruett poured her some water and lifted the cup to her lips and she sipped from it. "He died because of what I did."

"Not because of what you did," Pruett said. "Because of what some very bad people did—what they do for a living, Rachel. That is *not* on you. I'm a law officer. Do you think I would be here in this capacity—the role of a friend—if I thought any of this was your fault?"

This seemed to make her think, as she opened her bloodshot eyes and looked straight into Pruett's.

"But you know about before. What I did before."

"I did the same thing when I was younger. My wife forgave me. Tim would have forgiven you, dear."

"I'll never know. That's the part I can't live with."

"You can live with it," Pruett said. "People amaze themselves every day what they're capable of forgiving— even to themselves. You start there. You need to forgive yourself."

"I never will," she whispered.

"It feels that way," Pruett said, placing his hand lightly atop hers. "But things change, sweetie. I promise you. They change."

On the hour drive back to Wind River Pruett thought about nothing other than forgiveness. That, and being a hypocrite. How many times had he not forgiven himself? He didn't forgive himself now and didn't know that there was enough time left on his life calendar to accomplish such a task.

One of the first things Pruett learned in rehab was that a lie of omission was still a lie. Which meant he'd lied to his own team—the closest people to him. They knew *nothing*. And it was going to get worse. One lie begets another begets another.

He was already lying to the DEA. Fortunately he had an ally there; a friend who knew Pruett at the depths only few did. And the NTSB. At least there Pruett really didn't know anything. Let them figure out that the plane crashed into the mountain and went down into the crevasse.

Or whatever happened.

Pruett was worried about his team. Especially Baptiste. Pruett's and Baptiste's families went back. He'd eventually confide in Baptiste (if Malcolm hadn't already), but the waiting—the look in the deputy's eyes—it was restrained, but it was there. Red Horse Baptiste knew there was a lot more going on behind the Wizard's curtain.

The sheriff's final answer to himself? Doing what needed to be done. He'd convinced himself of that argument countless times. How could one not? If the ends were not justified then—well, then it was all a carnival ride, wasn't it? A cosmic joke. A universal blunder.

And James Pruett *the MAN* couldn't live if that were true.

So he'd done what he believed was necessary to preserve a way of life, a community, his own daughter, and what was right. Enrique had asked Pruett that very question: *did he believe in God*. Pruett had answered him "I believe in what's *right*."

Upon return to the station, there was a tension constricting the atmosphere. Baptiste was on patrol; Melody Munney was at her desk and did not look up at Pruett when he walked in; and Zach Canter looked like he'd swallowed a habanero pepper.

"Saw Rachel Shepard in case anyone's wondering," Pruett said as he walked to his office. "She's pretty damaged, inside and out. Guessing she could use some friends when she's released and gets back to town."

"Thanks, boss," Melody said.

Zach was silent as a priest in a cathouse.

Pruett dropped into his office seat, wondering what the hell was going on. He didn't have to wonder long. Zach Canter rapped on the open door.

"Zach," Pruett said. "Come on in and sit."

"May I close the door, Sheriff?"

"You do what you have to, son."

Canter closed the door and sat in the chair facing Pruett directly. "That envelope on your desk, it contains my resignation."

Pruett looked down at his desk, which appeared to have been hit by a helicopter downdraft. There was a brand new envelope right in plain view addressed to "Sheriff Pruett". Pruett left it where it lay.

"Well come right out and say it, Zachary."

"Sorry. I mean, I've been thinkin' about it all morning and decided the only way to tell you was to say it straight out."

"Like me," Pruett said, and grinned.

"Yeah, I guess so. Like you."

"I told you that morning you'd make a great sheriff, Zach. I meant it."

"That's what got me to thinkin'. Penny and I, we're going to try and have a baby."

"That's great, Zach. A lot of great cops have children, though."

"I know," Canter said. "And I love this job—you, Mel, Red Horse. You're like a second family to me."

"What's the real issue, son? You know we all care for ya, too."

Canter hesitated. "Penny's dad runs a business in Cody—a restaurant—it's been there for decades. He wants a partner and manager. Someone to take over the place one day."

"And he wants that to be you?" Pruett said.

"I want that to be me."

"Clearly you've thought this through. If I thought begging you would help, I would," said Pruett. "You're one of the finest deputy sheriffs I've ever had, Zach."

"I appreciate that, Sheriff."

"I'm askin' you to stay," said Pruett. "Just so you know."

"I know you are, sir."

"We'll miss you something fierce around here."

"I really do want this, Sheriff. I want you to know, this is *not* one of those 'bein' pressured' situations. It's a great move and somethin' I've thought about doin' for a long time. Ownin' a restaurant, I mean."

"I have no idea who said it, but someone did: it's the possibility of having a dream come true that makes life interesting."

"It's all in the letter," Zach said. "But you've been like a father to me. I mean that." Zach stood and left the office, saying he was taking his dinner break.

"You know about this?" Pruett called to Melody out in the bullpen.

She looked back at him, eyes glazed with tears and shrugged.

Chapter 14

PRUETT SPENT the next seventy-two hours dealing with both the DEA and the NTSB. As suspected, the NTSB simply needed his cooperation in answering any questions he and his team could answer regarding the debris field and the tail of the plane—also the report of the low-flying plane and why that did not register more concern in the sheriff than it did.

Nothing too serious that he couldn't handle.

But the DEA was a different situation altogether. Doug Hale was there—as Special Agent in Charge, in fact—but the primary questioning focused on the fact that it took Sheriff Pruett so long to report the attack at the Beard ranch.

"We didn't connect the dots there until after the incident at Stone Creek," Pruett told them. "Why would we?"

Doug did not perform any of the interviews. He left that to an Agent Clarence Jones, another black man. Doug had mentioned Jones before—thorough, by the book, but also a big believer in the good guys versus the bad guys and where that line should be drawn.

"Who else would you suspect of murdering everyone at the Beard Ranch, including livestock, and burning it to the ground?" Agent Jones had asked.

"As of now we're still running down leads," Pruett told him. "It's a local matter until I can figure it otherwise."

"And the 'incident' at Stone Creek? What made you think that had anything to do with the Beard murders?"

"I never said it did. I said it was after the incident, as in *on the timeline.* One of my deputies uncovered some names on a list he obtained at the ranger stations leading into the mountain trails. Horseback outfitters and riders are required to sign in and out. My deputy—Zach Canter— recognized a pair as being a relative of the Beards—who own mountain horses—and a local youth who is a climber."

"Back to Stone Creek. We've been pretty much stonewalled by the residents up there—those who allowed us onto their property at all. We were hoping you and your team might assist us in that part of the investigation."

"Happy to," Pruett had said. "For the record, though, I ain't too popular in that particular area and you won't be either. Those folks tend to be tight-lipped even with people they know and like."

"Are we talking racist tendencies? Just to be clear, I mean."

"Yep. Let's just say in the election that's not a part of the county I usually carry."

After a few more days of investigation, the NTSB ruled the crash and demise of unknown parties as accidental, due to the unpredictable nature of winds in the mountains (at least one plane crashed in the area every year, it seemed). The DEA also wrapped up its investigation around the same time. With no real evidence they marked their final report as "Unsolved" but included the theories Pruett was able to provide from Zach's end of the investigation. They also reported the decimation at the Beard ranch as "consistent" with other activities in Mexico and along the border, but all of it being circumstantial, there was ultimately no further they could go with the investigation.

Doug promised that he would be back up for a fly-fishing trip deep in the woods and that he and Pruett were long overdue for catching up, so Pruett knew he'd need to give his friend a more accurate debriefing, if not the entire truth.

Wendy had recovered and also had accepted Jay Hanson's proposal. They were planning on getting married in Wind River at a place yet undecided, the following summer. Pruett had been asked to give away the bride.

So things were finally beginning to settle down and Pruett had allowed himself the luxury of a bit of decompression when his cell phone sang to him. It was an unknown number and caller.

"Pruett," he answered.

"Sheriff Pruett," said a younger man with a thick Spanish accent.

"Yep. Who's this?"

"I think you know, Sheriff. Can we stop playing the games, as you say?"

"I know the organization you represent, but I don't know *you*. That leaves me at a disadvantage, sir."

"My name is Cristóbal Casales. Perhaps you know me now?"

"What's the nature of the call, Mr. Casales? I'll give us both the respect of assuming our message got sent and you received it."

"More than one message, I would say," said Casales.

"Okay."

"I want to meet with you," Casales said. "We have much to discuss."

"Maybe I don't see it that way."

"A wound is nothing. It is measured not by the breadth or the depth or even how much pain caused to the victim. A wound's import is determined by the scar it leaves."

"Now the man who doesn't like games is talking in riddles," Pruett said. "Enrique had a habit of speaking in riddles, though I didn't have the pleasure of his full acquaintance at the time."

"Enrique was a good man. He *did* have his eccentricities, but he served me well. This is why I want to talk to you. And believe me when I say this talk is the most important of your life, Sheriff. You sent a message—a wound. The size of the scar and who lives with such disfigurement depends on this conversation I am proposing."

"Very dramatic," said Pruett.

"I believe we started on the wrong foot," Cristóbal said. "Would you do me the honor of calling me Tóba? It is less formal and easier for conversation, no?"

"My name is James. Where and when would you like this meeting to take place?"

"I would like to see you tomorrow, James. In your town. You have nothing to fear—I come to this meeting alone. I must travel with my entourage, you understand, but you and I meet together at the place of your choosing, just the two of us."

"There's a place I like to eat, drink some coffee. I'll see what I can do about closing it down tomorrow. You understand *my* entourage will be outside. Just so we're clear."

"Then we agree, James. Tomorrow at noon?"

"High noon. I like that, Tóba."

"Enrique, he liked the old Westerns, no?"

"He did."

"This is no showdown, James. I just want to have a conversation. A very important one."

"Yep, got that the first time. I'll see you at noon, Tóba. I'll have an escort waiting for you at the local airport."

The plane that landed at the Wind River airport was big enough to hold its own Mercedes. The small airport could handle big planes; former Vice President Dick Cheney, who was from Wyoming and was partial to fly-fishing the rivers of the Green River valley, had landed in Air Force Two there more than once.

Three squad cruisers, driven by Deputies Red Horse Baptiste, Melody Munney, and Zach Canter, escorted Cristóbal's Mercedes into town, blue and red roller lights running the whole way. Ranchers lined the highway, unarmed, hands in their pockets, spitting chew on the ground.

The caravan arrived at the Wrangler Cafe without incident and Cristóbal Casales—future heir to the largest drug cartel and empire in the world—crossed the dusty parking lot in his white suit and entered the small diner.

"I brought you a gift," he said to Pruett who was at a table with his back to the wall, away from the windows. "May I sit?"

"Please, Tóba."

"You remember. Good, James. The gift, it is coffee. I have mine brought up straight from Guatemala—it is to die for, Sheriff."

"Already made us a pot. It'll do. But I appreciate the gesture just the same."

Casales nodded. "Very dramatic, our trip into town. You are a feisty bunch, you Wyoming people. Cowboys?"

"Some. Ranchers, we prefer to call 'em. But there are all manner of folk here, Tóba. Proud people. As in your town, I am sure."

"My country is a proud one indeed, James. This is why I understand what you did. The message you delivered told me a lot about you as a man."

"Let me pour you a cup," Pruett said, reaching for the decanter of coffee. "You take cream?"

"No whiskey? In Wyoming?" Cristóbal's bottomless black eyes remained fixed on Pruett's as he poured. "Let us partake of your local specialty as men."

"I don't drink anymore."

"Who does not drink, at least on special occasions?" Cristóbal said.

"Alcoholics," Pruett said, meeting Casales' stare head-on and with contained fury. He hated this cat and mouse shit.

"Yes I heard that," Casales said.

"Then why the fuck did you bring it up?" said Pruett.

"My apologies, James. I meant no offense. I brought coffee because I, too, am afflicted with a need to drink that turns my actions and my judgment, oh, how shall I put it? Not hospitable or forgiving. I asked about the drink because I wanted to see your reaction."

"There it is again with the games."

"Not a game, James. When I was younger, they called me *suero de la verdad*—loosely translated it is *finder of the truth*. The more accurate and technical translation is *truth serum*. Then it *was* just a game—a childhood contest. I would ask a boy or a girl one question to which I already knew the answer. The more personal, the better. If they tell me the truth, I know what that looks like. Same with the lie. I could always then tell if the second question I asked was being answered truthfully or not. I never lost."

"I'd not want to play poker with you," Pruett said.

"I have had success at this game, though I do not play much."

"We call 'em *tells*," the sheriff said, drinking his coffee.

"I have heard this term. Yes, tells. I am good at finding a person's tells. I was surprised to meet you, James."

"Yeah?"

"You are a black man in white man territory. A black man with a badge and gun, no less."

"If you knew our history better, Tóba, you'd know this ain't the white man's land any more'n it's mine. We both stole it from the Native Americans about a hundred and a half years ago."

"Yet it's called the *Winning of the West*," Casales said.

"By some. Not by me."

"Before we go on, James, I want to thank you for allowing my cousin, Omar, his freedom. His life."

"I don't start blood feuds. Had enough of 'em—they don't turn out well."

"In addition to being family—which is highly respected where I am from—he also has a wish. His son is in his twenties now and Omar has not seen him in quite a few years. He wishes to amend this wrong before he dies. Your grace has allowed this and I wanted you to know personally how much it is appreciated—by both myself, my father, and Omar."

"Personally I think the son is better off if that Omar monster never finds him," said Pruett.

"I respect you. I am told you speak from the heart. That is why I needed to meet with you face-to-face."

"You'll forgive me if I don't return the compliment, Tóba."

"I understand. You are a lawman first. That's largely why I respect you, as well as the message you sent to my people and me. We are not so different. I know this is cliché, but the truth of the matter is that men are built from a core. A seed. A nut from which we grow. One man makes a choice; the other, he chooses differently. But at the core, they can be the same."

"Not the same," Pruett said. "But yes, men can be very different and yet similar at the same time."

"Exactly. You and I have seen things. Done things. We leave it at that. But I realized I underestimated you. In fact I now see how much you expected me to do just that. Again, a mind to see the plan and a will to do what one must."

"I'm still not sure why you had to come all this way to say these things," Pruett said. "No disrespect intended."

"Because when I first received your message—the one you sent by murdering all of my men; good men, with families; burning all that money—I wanted to send a thousand of my finest soldiers to kill every man, woman, and child in this town and to burn it to ash."

"You were going to do that anyway," Pruett hissed.

"But this time it *would* have happened, cabrón. This is the way. To be the biggest—the *best*—as is Sustantivo, you must not disengage when a battle is lost. You exceed the other's victory."

"So what stopped you?"

"I have not said I stopped," Casales said. "And we find ourselves back at the beginning."

"I don't mind saying you lost me, Tóba."

"I have one more question for you, James."

"The finder of truth," Pruett said, a small, mirthless smile crawling across his mouth.

"Why did an honest man such as yourself take the last bag of money?"

"There is no other bag. All seven burned in that fire."

"Yes, the last communication I received from my people stated there were only seven. But trust me when I tell you here, there *were* eight bags. There have always been eight bags. Every flight."

"Never seen more than seven. If there's an eighth, it ain't here."

Cristóbal stared at Pruett and the sheriff felt afraid for the first time since meeting the drug lord. If there was a soul inside the man, it was a soul capable of things Pruett could not imagine.

"I believe you, amigo."

"A plane crash is a violent thing," Pruett said. "Maybe a bag landed in the front of the plane; the piece that fell down the crevasse. Of that much we're certain."

"Perhaps the other bag went, too. This is most likely, yes?"

"Yes."

"Was there a parachute discovered on board, Sheriff?"

"Yes. The pilot chute. A climber who came on the plane after the money was stolen took it as a souvenir. I can get it for you—"

"No. My curiosity only," Casales said. "I hope this is the last time we meet, Sheriff James Pruett, although in another life, well, we might have played poker."

"Are we good?"

"Qué? What do you mean?"

"I'd like to think that our accounts are even and that I won't be seeing any of your men in my town again."

"Yes, yes, we are even. I give you my word, James. My word is worth more than all the cartel's money, this I assure you."

Both men stood. Pruett extended his meaty paw and Casales gladly accepted it.

"Tóba," Pruett said and tipped his *Charlie 1 Horse* hat he'd never removed.

"I leave you the coffee, Sheriff. You will enjoy."

Chapter 15

THE LOG cabin Pruett and his wife Bethy built—which was really much more of a log *house* because of its size— was an honest labor of love, not a cliché. The land had been in the sheriff's family for over a hundred and fifty years. The particular parcel on which Pruett and his wife chose to build was near the family cemetery. None of the other descendants had built a home there, likely Pruett guessed—as he sipped on a rather delicious glass of lime sweet tea—because of the ghoulish nature of living so close to the dead.

Bethy and Pruett hadn't ever seen it that way. They'd planned on that spot being their dream home for decades before the first lumber was cut. For one thing, there wasn't a better view on the entire mountain—but that really wasn't it. Both the sheriff and his wife believed—as did most of the Native American tribes that populated the Pacific Northwest and the state of Wyoming—that ancestors were as important to the living now as when they'd been alive.

Each year Pruett sanded and repainted the white fence that surrounded the small cemetery. Of course Bethy was buried there now and one day he would join her.

Some days he felt he was closer than others.

Malcolm Whitefeather's arrival wasn't any surprise; Pruett had called him and asked him to come up.

"How's my favorite sheriff?" Whitefeather said as he climbed the porch steps stiffly.

"How many sheriffs you know?"

"Two," said the old Blackfoot Indian. "The other's dead. He ain't feelin' too good these days."

Whitefeather crossed the porch, sat down in the second chair, and poured himself a glass of tea. "Too bitter. Your wife was always better at makin' this stuff than you. One day I'll teach you my ancient Blackfoot recipe."

Pruett just stared at him. "You've never sat in that chair before," he said. "Not one time."

"She ain't in it anymore," Whitefeather said.

"That right?"

"Yep," said the old man and took another sip. "I could see that as I drove up. I think it's why you called me."

"I called you because I wanted to talk about everything that has happened."

"That's why *you* think you called. The spirits, they have other ideas."

"Hmm."

"I know these things. Bethy, she feels that you've let loose of her some. Trust me, it'll make the rest of her journey much easier."

"Can we get on with talking about what the spirits didn't really think I wanted to talk about?"

"Yep. How'd your talk with the big cheese from the cartel go?"

"I think it went okay. They're not coming back to Wind River."

"Or so they say."

"Weird thing," Pruett said. "I believed him."

"Sociopaths are believable, Jimmy. That's part of the deal."

"I know—I can't explain it. The cartel is done with our town."

"Unless another plane crashes here," Whitefeather said.

"Another plane with drug money crashes here, I officially retire. On that, you got my word."

"Amen."

"You heard anything from your people with the feds?"

"Not too many of my people work for the feds."

Pruett laughed. He loved the old geezer so much. Even in times of despair, when Pruett's heart felt as if it were going to shrink in on itself and never feel anything again, Mal could make him laugh.

"I ain't kiddin'," Whitefeather said. "My people mistrust the feds somethin' fierce."

"Mal."

"I heard their evidence is all circumstantial and there ain't gonna be any more of them damn thievin' feds around Wind River goin' forward."

"That's pretty much the same thing I heard," said Pruett.

"Then what in the Sam Hill am I doin' up here?"

"You said the spirits wanted you up here."

"Oh, hell, the spirits don't know what they want. I just needed you to feel better about me sittin' in Bethy's chair. My knees have been hurtin' me crazy-like lately. No way I coulda stood, leanin' on that uneven railing a yours."

"Uneven?"

"That railing slants to the east and I've been tellin' you that for *years*."

"That railing is fine. You need a new shtick."

"Don't say that. I'm a funny guy and I don't have many years left. Not enough to learn a new shtick, that's for certain."

"I spoke to Rachel up in the hospital. She's got a long road ahead, my friend."

"Did you speak to your daughter?" Whitefeather said. "Seems to me she's gonna have some trauma from this thing, too."

"'Course I talked to her," Pruett said. "Jay came down and picked her up; brought her back home to Laramie."

"*This* is her home," said Whitefeather.

"You know what I mean."

"She going to be okay?"

"She's getting married."

"That's a damned good thing."

"The spirits tell you that?"

"Matter of fact, they did."

Whitefeather put down his glass and stood. He put out his hand and Pruett shook it, strong and hard. "My knees are fine. Bethy, she's in a good place now."

"I know it."

"You better know it. Now we gotta start workin' on *you*," Whitefeather said and left the sheriff to his own thoughts.

He still didn't feel right about how everything went down. The plans, they worked. The feds might not be happy, but they were done with their investigating. Over the years since the wars, both literal and private—particularly since the loss of Bethy—Pruett had gotten pretty good at rebounding. This time was different. The strange thing? The animal inside was quiet. It was as if the blood violence had satisfied it for the time being and Pruett wasn't sure that made him feel better.

But at least he didn't want a drink.

He looked at the empty chair—the chair Mal Whitefeather had just occupied as if it were just another chair.

Then he picked up his phone and dialed Jesse.

Epilogue

THE CLIMATE in Israel took some getting used to, even after a few months, but Mark had a very specific and operationally sound plan for moving around the globe. After Israel was Rio de Janeiro in nine more months, then every year a different city in the world, always paying cash. Once he felt that he was relatively safe (his estimate was five cities, five years, but he was not an idiot: he knew he'd be looking over his shoulder for the rest of his life—until he was eighty-nine and on his deathbed, even; this was a simple reality he'd come to accept). But his plan—his only hope at living off the money—was constant movement for a time, and living cheaply.

Most countries had relatively flexible tourist laws, allowing a person with a valid passport between six months and a year to "visit" before getting nosey about said tourist's reason for still pandering around (in most countries, not unlike the United States, once you were in, the amount of time varied in concert with the individual's ability to stay below the scanning light of detection).

After sending DEA Agent Palo out of the plane—after committing murder against a federal agent—Mark Coulee circled the lake until the idea burst in his mind as if it had been contained within a clear bubble that unexpectedly burped up from his gray matter: *the autopilot*. Mark had already engaged it when trying to push the dying Palo from the Cessna and was then using it to circle the lake but the capabilities of the state-of-the-art system, depending on weather conditions, wind shear, and other variables, could literally land an aircraft within a radius of ten feet or less. The Wind River Range was full of well-marked crevasses that could swallow a Cessna 172 as easily as a whale swallows plankton. He realized he *knew* of a crevasse that would be perfect—Solomon's Crevasse. Solomon's was one of the several dozen primary crevasses that even had GPS coordinates for hikers and tourists to locate them while visiting the mountain range.

And Solomon's—like many of the larger crevasses—was considered "bottomless" (which simply meant it was so deep no one had ever been able to reach its lowest point). The craterous mouth of such a hole in the earth was enormous. If Mark got the plane close enough and high enough he could program the geo coordinates of the crevasse into the system, which would send the plane down to the bottom where no one would find it again, and once the coordinates were programmed, Mark could manually fly the aircraft to an area above the tree line, hopefully in a semi-level rock or earthen field, engage the autopilot for a few minutes of level flight before the secondary destination of the crevasse took over, and parachute to hopeful safety. He would only be able to handle one of the bags of cash, but that was three and a half million dollars and did not include the money he'd distributed amongst various foreign bank accounts. If he survived—which was in no way guaranteed—he'd have at least a dozen miles to hike out of the mountains down into town, but from there he could buy a vehicle for cash, drive to Jackson Hole and fly to Denver or Los Angeles or San Francisco where he'd spend a day or so cleaning out his accounts in the Bahamas, Canada, and Switzerland.

The one risk Mark figured he had to accept was the creation of a new, verifiable passport. He was now ostensibly being looked for by the feds for murder (assuming Palo's body were ever found and determined to be a homicide—Mark chose to take the worst case view) and, of course, the cartel, neither organization of which were known for giving up their searches.

He reached out to a friend from the Navy who he knew had connections for such difficult yet authentic items. His friend lived in Lakewood, California so Mark chose a flight to Los Angeles and was fortunate enough to arrange a new document—the downside: it took a week. Mark had never spent seven more terror-filled days, not even in the Iraq war. He stayed in his room with a 9 MM pistol he borrowed from his friend under his pillow—well, sleep was an overstatement; he dozed off between real and imagined noises in the night.

The passport also cost him twenty-three thousand dollars but it was virtually indistinguishable from a true international passport. The document listed his country of origin as Belgium and showed him as having modestly travelled throughout the world, including two trips to the United States as a tourist (two weeks each visit, once to New York, once—his latest trip—to Los Angeles).

His new name was Johan De Vos and his plan was to retire in the Netherlands—most likely in Amsterdam (not an unusual thing for a Dutch-speaking Belgian to do). Johan De Vos was also practicing Flemish Dutch in his spare time and found that he had quite a knack, thanks to Rosetta Stone software and an undiscovered talent at vocal mimicry.

It had been months and Mark was still having nightmares—not of the cartel or police following him but of the murder of Palo. Mark relived that moment over and over in his sleep. It did not matter who Palo was; Mark had not signed up to be a murderer. His execution of Sammy he considered a mercy killing and his brain had somehow locked the event away to torture him at another time in a different way.

But it had been *his* decision to kill Palo in cold blood. He knew nothing of the man—Palo could have had a wife and children; he could have been a soccer coach with a team of young boys and girls excitedly awaiting his return.

Mark had stolen the only thing that really mattered to a person—his future and everything in it. And that was the overarching thought pounding his brain and tearing apart his heart.

Clint Eastwood said, as William Munney in *Unforgiven*:
You take away all he has and all he's ever gonna have.

The money meant less and less to Mark, as did his freedom.

He had a choice. He could have landed in Canada and stolen out from there. He could have completed the mission and prayed Cristóbal did not suspect him of anything, taking his chances.

Mark sipped on an espresso. His hand was shaking, making the cup difficult to hold. He was a mess. Sleep-deprived.

He was considering calling Tóba. He could lie. Say he survived the plane crash and was delirious—not knowing whose money he'd found he took just one bag, keeping it until he remembered who he was.

He could call the sheriff of that small town— what was it? —Wind River. Find out if they found Palo; if he was okay. Perhaps Mark was not a murderer after all. He finished his drink. He was going insane. If he didn't get some sleep soon he was either going to die or he was going to slip up, which meant the same thing.

Then he felt the huge, simian hand grip his shoulder and the deep, (perhaps) brotherly voice speak his name:

"Marcus—"
And Mark wept.

ABOUT THE AUTHOR

R.S. Guthrie grew up in Iowa and Wyoming. He has been writing fiction, essays, short stories, and lyrics since college.

"Black Beast: A Detective Bobby Mac Thriller (Volume 1)" marked Guthrie's first major release and it heralded the first in a series of Detective Bobby Mac books. The second in the series (Lost: A Detective Bobby Mac Thriller (Volume 2) hit the shelves December of 2011.

Guthrie's "Blood Land" is the first in the *James Pruett Mystery* series and represents a project that is close to his heart: it is set in a fictional town in the same Wyoming where he spent much of his childhood and still visits.

This sequel, "Money Land" released at the end of 2012 and the author is working on the third in the series, "Honor Land", which is scheduled for release in the Spring of 2013.

Guthrie lives in the Colorado Rockies with his wife, Amy, three young Australian Shepherds, and a Chihuahua who thinks she is a 40-pound Aussie!

Readers can catch up with what's new with the author at his official site, http://www.rsguthrie.com , discussions related to writing and other topics at his blog, Rob on Writing (http://robonwriting.com) or at his showcase of authors giving back to causes at the Read A Book Make A Difference (RABMAD) website: (http://RABMAD.com/authors).

Other books by R.S. Guthrie

<u>Sheriff James Pruett Mystery / Thrillers:</u>

Blood Land
Money Land
Honor Land

<u>Detective Bobby Mac Mystery / Thrillers:</u>

Black Beast
L O S T
Reckoning

<u>Non-Fiction:</u>

INK: Eight Rules To A Better Book

www.ingramcontent.com/pod-product-compliance
Lightning Source LLC
Chambersburg PA
CBHW060148130626
46556CB00006B/2545